SAIL

SAIL

... taking tall ships across the oceans

John Idris Jones

Blanche Currie, built in *Borth-y-Gest*, 1875

JOHN JONES

Published by John Jones Publishing Ltd.,
Borthwen, Llanfair Road, Ruthin, Dinbych LL15 1DA

Printed and bound in Wales by
Gomer Press, Llandysul, Ceredigion SA44 4JL

Dedicated to those remarkable men who designed
Porthmadog/Borth y Gest ships, to those craftsmen
who built them, to those brave men who sailed
them huge distances and to those who went down,
never to come back home.

EXCELSIOR
PRIDE OF WALES
FLEETWING
BLANCHE CURREY
C.E.SPOONER
DOROTHY
BLODWEN
CARL AND LOUISE
M.A.JAMES
R.J.OWENS
GESTIANA

Cilan, Borth y Gest

We drove from the Berwyns, those closed-in mountains, and as we passed through Porthmadog and turned up the narrow road behind it, through Y Garth and past Sybil Thorndike's house (Bron-y-Garth), we had a competition on the first to see *taid's* (grandfather's) house and cry out "Cilan".

My grandparents had built the house for their retirement in the year I was born, 1938. I have pictures showing a tubby baby boy in my mother's arms by the leaded-glass front door, and standing with a sturdy posture on the earth patch that was to become the front lawn, the masts of yachts visible behind me.

The garden was grandfather's joy. He was out early, hoeing and planting, growing potatoes, erecting the cane poles, strung together like teepees, for his sweet peas, and creating liquid manure in a large tin container. When I went down to play with my friends, he would stand at the edge of the lawn and make a distinctive whistle to bring me back for my meal – *cinio* – lunch. My boat – a skiff of varnished wood – would then be pulled-up on the bank next to Tai Pilots, and I would make my way to Cilan around the curving road, over the little stream and the well-worn rocks and through Cilan's small front gate.

The house faced the sea; all was light and air except for the storms in the winter when the gusts of wind were so fierce that they cracked the windows in the front bedrooms.

I was particularly fascinated by the attic. I spent many hours there, sitting by the table inside the dormer window that looked out over the bay and over the estuary towards the open sea. The curve of small houses were as a necklace around the bay and the sand changed colour from light to dark as it warmed between the sea's encroaches.

Access to the attic was via a wooden trapdoor in the landing's ceiling; you took a wooden pole with a brass ferrule, hooked it in place and pulled down. The steps came down and I rose carefully, as if I was a sailor climbing up the ropes to adjust the sails.

For a year, I attended Junior School which was located at the head of the street ascending the hill opposite Cilan. It had a monkey-puzzle tree at the front, and there I recall learning the poem *Abw Ben Adhem* and been clouted on the ear for whistling in the washroom during a toilet break from lessons.

Each day I went home from school across the sands of the bay, if it was dry, and when the tide was in, around the road, past Borthwen, a house at the end of the row, which was a dairy, where our milk came from.

Taid was Master of the house; it was his ship. He dominated the kitchen. The high-point of his year was at Christmas when he made treacle toffee (*cyflath*, as he called it). The gas cooker, in the corner of the back kitchen was his galley, and the toffee emerged in tin trays, covered in a light sprinkling of castor sugar. When cooled, I was given a small metal hammer to break it up; it was handed-around the family with a certain reverence.

On the wall of the kitchen was a painting of a sailing ship. It had a gold-coloured frame. The sea at the bottom had white tops to the waves and a rowing-boat at the left. She appeared to be sailing in to a harbour. I read later that Italian artists had a business in painting ships, which would be bought by the captain of the vessel, and hung with pride in their homes. The ship had three masts. The sky was blue. From the foremast hung a series of so-called square sails. The main mast carried fore-and-aft sails, as did the mizzen (the aftermost). In later years, I looked more carefully at the writing at the bottom. It said she was the *Blanche Currie*.

What happened to the painting? I do not know. It must be somewhere, hanging on some wall in somebody's house. I have no sentiment about the painting, but I value her picture in my mind, as part of my childhood. The house and its contents have gone out of the family. But the tide of memory remains. It sweeps from the past in to us. It runs through us in a creative sweep, making, creating and destroying, as does the sea.

And what I did not know then was that this ship was built (in 1875) some two hundred yards from my grandfather's house, on the bay-edge space used by ship builder Richard Jones of Garreg Wen. And as I walked down the path to play with my friends, or walked to school across the Borth y Gest bay, or walked back to Cilan at my grandfather's whistle, I was stepping on the stones and slate ridges that originally held the *Blanche Currey* as she grew to life-form.

Chapter 1

TOPSY was in full steam. She chuff-chuffed along with a streak of steam flowing from her brass chimney.

All eyes were on her. Faces were tilted downwards to watch this miracle of engineering.

As the miniature locomotive made the long loop around the edge of the garden at Bron-y-Garth, faces moved in unison to the left and then to the right. She was running on a pair of rails a mere three and one-eighth inch gauge.

William Williams was standing proudly, the buttons on his waistcoat prominent as he tucked his thumbs in to the lower pockets. He was wearing his best suit for this, a very special occasion.

"Just a little mover. She is the perfect engine. She has the power," he muttered to himself in Welsh as the work of his hands displayed her excellence.

He was a maker; a hands-on man. He was not an accountant or an owner. He was not as Charles Easton Spooner and Spooner's father. He – William – was an engineer. He was a man who bent over a piece of hot iron and knew that out of it he could make a wheel. He knew that by mixing them in the correct proportions that brass, copper and tin would meld together to make a locomotive. And, given the wood and able carpenters, carriages, trolleys and vans could be built by hand.

He raised his eyes over the neatly-trimmed shrubs and over the garden wall. Beyond was the panorama that he was used to. Snowdon over the left; Cnicht and the Moelwyns straight ahead and in the foreground the blue waters of the Bay of Porthmadog, where the rivers Dwyryd and Glaslyn combined. Beyond these ever-changing waters was the shoreline of Meirionnydd with Harlech castle, and beyond that, out to sea, was a faint long smudge marking the bar, where dangerous tumbling waters marked the end of the Bay and the beginning of the long ocean.

As he looked, the top half of a schooner came in to view. She was three-masted, with four square sails on her foremast, a serious ship for the serious ocean. Built by hand from local labour, she was making her confident way out to sea. 'Carrying slate,' he thought, 'She looks in her element. Fast and stable. This is what the schooners are built for.'

Sail out. Steam in. He saw himself as an engineer in metal; a man of making things that had a specific task in the improvement of man. He glanced at the sailing ship again. Certainly she was handsome. But she relied on man's labour, on the hoisting of sails to catch the wind, on turning the wheel to direct her, and in her birth, the huge effort needed to build her.

But I look for labour without man in the future, he thought. I make machines and they will generate enough power to carry hundreds of men to their work. That is the past – he looked again at the ship – and I am the future.

He turned back to the gathering on the lawn. His son Johnnie tugged at his trousers. Johnnie pointed to where the three inch gauge track had been pushed out of line by someone's shoe. "*Rhoi o'n ôl*," William instructed to his son. Johnnie, as the engineer-in-making he was (he was later to work on the East Bengal Railway, India) moved over to where the track was bent and re-set it, pushing the steel stakes in soundly.

Charles Easton Spooner was the owner of Bron-y-Garth and he was a proud man. He had overcome the obstacles and he was about to see the Festiniog Railway come in to its own, fare-carrying, reliable, profitable. He stood on the terrace in the upper part of the front garden, somewhat solitary. The terrace was edged with a stone construction, knee height, of uprights and cross-pieces. The house itself has a lop-sided character, with large window bays on the Porthmadog side, but not on the Borth y Gest side.

Charles had lost his dear wife Mary Elizabeth to typhoid some five years ago and were it not for the presence of his sister Louisa, his life would be empty indeed. Empty but for the ambition. It was his overwhelming desire to see the railway well established, with its own rolling stock made by its own foundry and works, running up to and from Blaenau, carrying slate. He looked at William Williams. He saw a man after himself but with other skills, without the social additions.

"Father, what a beautiful day," said the youngest of his three sons, Charles Edwin. "We are having a good time. What a marvellous engine. And William Williams made it all himself. Do you know, he made his own tools for the job."

"Yes, I did know. He must have very good eyesight."

The little train, about the size of a terrier dog, continued its chuff-chuffing around the garden. It zipped across the X-shaped junctions and stopped under the signals. As it chuffed away confidently, John stepped forward holding a miniature shovel. He thrust it in to the base of the tender and a small shovel-full of ground-up coal was thrown into the fire which momentarily puffed out a flame of fire.

"A really amazing thing," said Charles Edwin. "I don't suppose there is anything like it in the world."

"I think not," replied his father, turning his face upwards, revealing his square bushy beard. He had the greatest respect for William Williams, his Superintendent of Railways.

In another part of the garden another man of the upper sort was stationed next to his wife. David Williams was a solicitor and Member of Parliament for Meirionnydd. He took the Welsh bardic name of *Dewi Heli*. He was controller of the Madocks estate. Naturally, he owned property.

He had a curious manner. His eyes resembled the top halves of two boiled eggs, protruding, observing, summing up. He had a mind for gain. When he saw a weakness, it became an opportunity, and he moved in with charm and deference, emerging with advantage.

One of his attributes was fertility. He had impregnated his wife Annie with a regularity in tune with the calendar and three of his children were here today, on this sunny headland above the Glaslyn. It was to his advantage to be close to Charles Spooner. Much legal business was necessary. The Festiniog Railway was steaming ahead and there was money to be made. Slate was at the heart of it. Heavy, everlasting slate, the world's best substance for covering new roofs. It had to be mined, carried to the port and sent abroad, by sail. Germany was mad for it. Slate was our gold.

An important man needs a son. His son, Arthur Osmond was 20 and a handsome young man. He must be in need of a wife. His father's eyes moved around the garden, from finery to finery.

Arthur Osmond was looking too. But no finery caught his eye. He saw the three young men under the yew tree.

His sisters Florence (the elder, aged fifteen) and Blanche (age fourteen) stood together, and very attractive they looked. They were dressed by a dressmaker in Caernarfon and a shoe-maker in Criccieth. Florence wore black shoes; Blanche wore brown calf laced half-boots. Blanche generally liked the plainer look: her dress was sharply cut above the bosom. Florence wore a silken brown dress with lace over the shoulders.

"This is a beautiful house," said Florence. "To have the view of the estuary in the morning and to see the sun going down over the horizon in the evening."

Blanche was not so impressed. "I like the woods and fields that we have. I like to see things that grow."

They both glanced across the garden at the three young men.

The three boys of Charles Easton Spooner stood in a

cluster under the yew tree: Charles Edwin, John Eryri and George Percival. At first glance, each seemed handsome, but on closer inspection, John did not stand up because there was a curious stiffness about his face and body, almost as if he had not quite mastered the craft of standing up. Charles Edwin was undeniably handsome, with a lean body, close-cut hair, a craggy face with moustache and a long sharp nose. He wore a suit of plain mid-grey. Percy was chubbier, of lower height, but possessed of the charm of the natural *bon viveur*. He was wearing a suit of mid-blue marked by a check of smoky white.

"My dear Charles, old chap," said Percy, "it's time we had a decent drink." It was generally thought that drink came naturally to Percy; his father had frequently sniffed, and warned him of the dangers.

"We must contact the kitchen," replied Charles in his low, controlled, tone.

A few minutes later, a young woman came towards them with a tray holding three cut-glass wine-glasses and a honey-coloured bottle of white wine, with the cork lying beside it. Quite right for the occasion, thought Charles. The young lady came closer. She was dressed in a pinafore and collar but the hem of her dress, and her shoulders, were embraced with a cloth displaying a sparkle of silver against a background of light blue. It was the colour of the sea, decorated with exotic fish. It was a combination that drew Percy's eyes. Her eyes, too, were blue, under a wave of golden hair which swept across her forehead.

"Very good," said Charles, moving the glass to his mouth.

"Yes," murmured Percy. "Yes, most kind." His manner was unusually subdued, but his eyes were set on the young lady before him.

By this time, the miniature train had come to a halt. Applause came from the gathering. Willliam Williams, smaller in stature than the men present, stepped forward and took a modest bow.

"Excellent. Excellent." announced Charles Easton. "We have seen the future. Wonderful." He smiled at William Williams, who was stepping forward with a brown tarpaulin. He folded it in half and laid it on the ground.

He stepped back. The engine was heavy and hot. He looked towards Percy who raised a hand at him.

The two men kept the engine upright by sliding a metal rule through it, lifting it up and placing it down in the centre of the tarpaulin. They raised the sides of the tarpaulin so that the hot parts of the engine were not close to their hands. They raised the tarpaulin with its contents together and walked with her out of the garden, William's young son walking proudly with them. Only Percy, of all the men in the garden that fine day, would have been asked to help William with his unique engine, for Percy was a railway man.

He was talented, they knew that here; and they knew it down in the railway workshops. He drew on his father's skill in planning and drawing. But, unlike many young men of his class, he did not mind getting his hands dirty. When needed, he was a hands-on man.

He was shortly to become a hands-on man in another way too.

As he walked out of the garden with William Williams, carrying the miraculous engine, he looked backwards towards the kitchen. His mind was full of the creature he had just seen, her hands holding the glass and the gold of her hair glinting in the sun.

And as a consequence, his involvement with railway engines and companies was to take him to a far-away place, where he was to deal with people more foreign than his colleagues and work-mates in a corner of Porthmadog.

Chapter 2

SHON EDWARDS, in the early Spring of 1870, was hard at work making his ideal woman. He and his father occupied Tan-y-Graig, Criccieth, and they were both wood-men. His father, with his strong brown hands and tufts of hair over his ears, one of which almost permanently covered a flat pencil typical of his trade, had all his life made doors, windows, floors, joists and so on, being the essential pieces for building houses. He was an artisan, and a very good one. He was almost never out of work, and his services were required all across Meirionnydd. But he was also an artist. Even a pig-sty behind a house received his careful attention: something about the door and frame spoke of the work of Tomos Edwards, joiner. He never made an ugly thing in his life. And as is often the case, what was in the father was also in the son, but more so. In the son, the artistic became developed, refined.

If his father made wood that joined, that was necessary for domestic life, so his son made wood that spoke for itself, that possessed symbolism and metaphor. This time, he was in his element. Symbolism was in the drawings. He had twenty pages of them. Shon's black pencil and carbon stick had traced out the swirling shapes of the Indies, the Far East, in shapes of jungle animals, flying birds, of the insects of the Burma forest and the elephants of the Punjab.

But now he had a different challenge, to finish off the *Pride of Wales* with a design for her prow. A process of making which took a real human being and replicated her in wood and paint. A process of sculpting a woman yet not a woman. Of making a female in wood which represented a shape which stayed long in the mind after the ship she fronted had gone away on the high seas. On land, as he was, she was not company; at sea, on the moving ocean, she was company to the sailors who toiled behind her. She was sister, friend and lover; in the minds of sailors far from land the figurehead was a reminder of the human world they had left behind.

She was to be the figurehead of the new ship, a barque, *Pride of Wales*, being built at Borth y Gest. Shon's drawings – swirling, exotic, mysterious – were to be painted on the ship as a tribute to her calling on the Indian Ocean, her destination.

Mother had died of TB some six years previously and both men missed her dearly. She had been the star of the household, hard-working, diligent, God-fearing and devoted to her two men, especially her son with his large eyes, narrow shoulders and polite manner. At school, Shon created drawings which were the envy of his peers and the wonder of his teachers. Out of nothing, apparently, he could create buildings, landscapes, animals, with his pen with no first efforts; they just flowed from him. And when it came to ships, it was as if he was born for this task. He could draw a schooner or brig with a precision and accuracy down to the last inch. His speciality was sails. He loved the size and the energy of sails. He loved their movement and the way they negotiated with the wind to create an energy that was useful out of a set of movements which were beautiful. That was how it was in the wind, but the trick Shon Edwards had at his finger-tips was the translation of that energy and beauty in to a drawing that was two-dimensional. The three-dimensional real ship was being built in Borth y Gest, Shon's drawings were anticipated with pleasure; and the work of his hands in making a figurehead for the fine new ship was talked about by many who worked and lived here

He was in his father's house and he was working. Before him, now upright, was the woman emerging.

His father knew that his talented son was creating something special. Shon did not like visitors to his room when he was working. So at night, his son asleep, Tomos crept downstairs and opened the door of the workroom. He did not light a candle or a lamp because usually the moonlight coming in through the window was enough to show how the work was progressing. He stood there for five minutes in silent contemplation of the work in progress. He had admired the shape of the body, one leg forward, the shaped bust and the turn of the shoulder. Then, at a later visit, he saw the legs take shape and he saw the arms with their muscle and femininity.

Pride of Wales was a barque, perhaps the most beautiful of ships. Her three masts were majestic: from each of the foremast and the main mast hung five square sails. The bottom sails (course) were huge and caught the wind with a pronounced ballooning. Above them on the two masts hung sails which angled up to the smallest, the sky sail. The rear mast, the mizzen, usually carried a pair of fore-and-aft sails. But when in ambitious mode, this mizzen carried five square sails. So she could feature fifteen square sails. In between these three sets of sails hung four stay sails, like handkerchiefs. This multiplicity of sails in practice on the water becomes a power-fused unity and the appearance of such a ship when moving is magnificent. She was adaptable, capacious, very fast and looked stunning. At 300 tons and 125 feet long she was bigger than any boat previously built on this shoreline of Caernarfonshire. She was indeed the pride of Wales.

The following day there was a knock at the door. Shon opened it and found before him a tall man wearing a brown suit. It was Simon Jones, designer and builder of ships.

"My boy," said Simon, stretching out his hand. "You look a little tired. Is it going well?"

"Yes," said Shon, if a little hesitantly. "I have finished the drawings. Now I am on the woman."

"On the woman!" repeated Simon. "That's a good one. Be careful you do not get carried away, or there'll be a price to pay."

Shon laughed. "I think she's coming on well."

Simon had an envelope in his hand. He passed it to Shon. "Something to keep you going. Five guineas."

He handed Shon a ledger page with the amount entered. In the space next to the figure Shon wrote his signature.

Simon looked up in to Shon's eyes. "Can I see her?"

Shon took a step back and there was a pause.

"I'd like to get on more before I show her."

Simon was disappointed, but he understood the artistic temperament, the secret relationship between carver and subject.

"Perhaps next week," said Shon.

"I'll be back," said Simon as he turned to go. He glanced back at the house and he felt the isolation of the two men, one of whom had lost a woman, the other was busy creating one. When there is something lost, there is usually something gained, thought Simon.

Chapter 3

LOUISA SPOONER was very much the captain of this
ship. Bron-y-Garth was like a ship, positioned within
yards of the sea, looking over the estuary and out towards
the Atlantic. And all had to be ship-shape: for was not her
brother an important man? A man who had stuck through
it through thick and thin. A man who had driven the idea
of the railway with tenacity and ambition. It was no easy
thing that he had done and was still doing. This railway
was a world first. He was close to seeing the Festiniog
Railway come to the point of its fruition, with locomotives
and carriages carrying passengers up and down the little
line from Porthmadog to Blaenau Festiniog and back. He
had released the slate industry from its bottleneck along the
Dwyryd to how it was now, with slates carried to the new
quay at Porthmadog by steam train on the narrow railway.

No doubt, it had been a hard slog. And Louisa saw it in his
eyes that things were telling on him. No longer the laugh,
the vigour. His beard had grown whiter and his eyelashes
wilder. But he still has it in him, he thought. There was a
space around him where there used to be connection. The
boys were a group and there was a separation between them
and their father. Each one was more likely to be talked to
brusquely, even shouted at, rather than spoken to in soft,
fatherly, terms.

And this day, the vigour and the placidity were there
together. William Williams of the Festiniog Railway was
there with his son, the father proud and strong. Here, at
home, the three boys were beginning to make lives for
themselves. The two Williams girls from Castell Deudraeth

were attractive in their finery and ready for womanhood. The young people were showing an interest in each other. But Charles Easton Spooner, owner of this house, patriarch, had something missing. No longer the jovial host; he observed but did not respond with ebullience. His conversation was selective and short.

He will never, thought Louisa, get over the loss of his beloved Mary Elizabeth. She had died of typhoid early in 1864. And to add further injury, her nurse Elizabeth Price, died two days later. Louisa knew that the household was devastated. That no longer would be the concerned voice and the purposeful movement. No longer the talk of the new day at breakfast. When you lose somebody, the gap in the air is never filled.

Louisa felt the responsibility. She had come here at her brother's invitation, to be mistress of the household, with its six bedrooms, long sitting-room, dining-room with its polished mahogany table – extended when there were guests at dinner – and kitchen with its black double grate and oak table.

She had chosen a new cook. She was determined to run the household in the best fashion. She also decided on two new maids, one for the kitchen and one for the rooms. She laid down methods and routines. It was all to be spick and span; he brother deserved the best. Even Eleanor Davies, the new maid, was shaping up. She had been slow to learn but now she possessed a routine which saw greater poise and production in her.

Louisa looked out of the kitchen window. The side of the house she looked at backed upon Trwyn Cae Iago, the headland between this house and the inlet of Borth y Gest. There were bushes and trees growing wild and no-one quite know where the edge of the estate was; on the sea side, it ran along the cliffs that rose over the shoreline, with its black slate faces and serrated edges. Down there, on this headland there were small bays and caves; where a number of ships had come to grief in vicious gales.

She had told the head gardener, Dafydd Davis, that all this woodland and wild stuff ought to be cut and trimmed, so that one could walk in the woods. He had taken on a new man who had some experience of timber. She saw him looking at a tree, working out how to tame it. Davis was now close to the house, forking one of the flower beds. He looked up and their eyes met. He made a faint gesture, sufficient to acknowledge that she was a Spooner but not the owner.

"Huummm," muttered Louisa, turning away from the window. She had a habit of uttering non-word sounds. She was not sure that her efforts to improve the garden on this wild side of the house were being put in to practice.

"Ma'am, the young men are asking for drinks," said Eleanor. "What shall I serve?"

Luisa was about to say – the usual lemonade, but then she thought that this was a special occasion. She replied, "Go down to the cellar. The white French are on the right. Bring one of the Sauterne."

This was something new to Eleanor. The cold of the cellar touched her face as she stepped carefully down the stone steps. She lit a candle. The labels on old paper attached to the frames were hard to read but she saw the cleaner bottoms of the newer bottles, thinking that this was not a dinner party that would need the dustier bottomed, more expensive, wines. She spotted the letters 'Sau' and removed a bottle. Upstairs, showing it to Louisa, she had the pleasure of seeing she had selected correctly.

"Draw the cork?" said Louisa.

"Never done it before, ma'am," she replied.

"See," said Louisa. "This way."

She peeled away the covering, inserted the old corkscrew with the bone handle, and in two jerks, which involved her underarm, the cork came away.

"So, you learn," said Louisa.

The sun was shining as Eleanor took the bottle with three

glasses to the Spooner sons under the yew tree. She was pleased she was learning these new things.

"Splendid," said Charles. "Wine this time. How delicious."

"Shall I pour?" said Eleanor. Receiving approval, she poured the wine carefully in to the three hand-held glasses.

There was a sparkle in the air. Eleanor had brought it. As she turned to leave, leaving the tray and bottle on the garden table, the line of her body with its tulip-shaped thigh attracted attention, especially Percival's.

Percy was taken by her. He was at the beginning of a fascination which was to become a passion. He felt the pull of her; of her body and spirit. His eyes followed her outline, and the way she moved stayed with him. She had a rhythm which started as a faint music and then enlarged itself as the weeks passed so that it became powerful and insistent.

Eleanor was enjoying the day. She was being introduced to the way things were done here. It was all new to her but she did not feel cowed. She felt she fitted-in; she did not feel inferior. She was stepping-up a class and her new life was convivial. She returned to the kitchen with a half-smile on her face and a distant look, as if knowing that her life was to change, and that she could handle the change.

Chapter 4

FIVE SHIPBUILDING men in waistcoats sat on a pine plank watching the activities in the harbour.

Harry Davis was holding a newspaper.

"Emigration to Argentina," he read aloud.

"What does the paper say? That we should emigrate?" said Ted, the youngest.

"Emigrate to America," chipped in Amos Jones, not the brightest of the five. "We can sit in a bar in 'Frisco and drink boo-bonn."

"Bourbon. American whisky. Jack Daniels. He was a Welshman." Harry was one for correcting, and had good information.

"One that got away," said Ted, who was ambitious and was prepared to travel. "Making money in the States."

"But Argentina," said Harry. "That's a long way."

"Get in a schooner, point her westwards and fly away." Amos's faith in schooners came to near magical proportions.

"They sailed in the *Mimosa*," read Harry.

"What's that?" said Ted.

"Never heard of her," said Gareth. "A schooner? A brig?

Harry looked closely at the newspaper. "A tea clipper, it says here."

"A clipper," two of them said in unison. "A tea clipper. What a vessel. For crossing the Atlantic all the way to Argentina. Are they mad?"

The consensus was that a clipper was a bad idea.

Three masted but carrying a small footage of canvas. No large fore-and-aft sails. No tall masts. Nothing to catch the Atlantic winds and drive her forward. A slow ship. Wide bellied. It needed the gaff right up on the mizzen to raise the largest sail, and all the other sails hung from yardarms, needing constant hoisting and adjustments. A ship built for hugging the coastline, for turning corners, not for sailing over mighty seas.

"And how many people on board?" asked Ted.

Harry looked again at the paper, "One hundred and fifty."

"One hundred and fifty," they said again in unison. "What! Overcrowding, my God. They'll be sleeping in turns. The food! The children! The lavatories!

They looked around them. Porthmadog was home. A safe place. For a moment they inwardly prayed for their countrymen on board the *Mimosa*.

"Is there a preacher on board?" asked Ted.

Harry looked at his paper again. "Yes. One."

"He will be needed. For funerals."

"This place they are going to," asked Will Roberts. "Will it be like Blaenau Ffestiniog?"

"Yes. Quite similar. Windy. Rocky. Barren," replied Ted.

"I have relatives going on this trip. John and Mary Roberts and their two children. Of Bwthyn Bach, Llan Festiniog. They are going for a better life." Will was genuinely concerned.

"Led by preachers. Hoping to God. There are people who can be persuaded into anything," said Harry. "There are people going from Rhosllanerchrugog, I see. The place is full of chapels."

"And mines. Holes in the ground. Dark. Dark. I couldn't do it. Give me the air, the light. Give me clouds over my head." Will looked around him. "The wind in the sails. I don't want to be in a dark hole."

The prospects. The better life. The people of Rhos and Porthmadog were tied to improvement, searching for income, security and a good future for their children.

In the sunshine on the quay the five men replaced the lids of their food tins, emptied the dregs from their tin cups, drew their studded boots on the slated ground and rose to return to work.

Chapter 5

EBENEZER ROBERTS was a ship-builder. He had learned his trade with Henry Jones in the 1840s: Henry Jones had a near-mystical reputation, building on Canol y Clwt, which became Greaves Wharf. He was one of those rare men who combined energy with a quality of practical imagination that caused the mind to skip over details and arrive at a conclusion which was invariably correct. He could imagine a ship, in all its details, before it was built. A shape in his imagination guided his instructions to his men as the building took place. He did not need to work from a plan on paper or a model. 'Harry' they called him, and the shadow of this man spread forward over all the shipbuilding that was to take place in Porthmadog in the nineteenth century.

Ebenezer took on some of this quality, but the stereotype had already been established, so the work was not based on a new design but on one established in Henry's day. But Ebenezer took the matter forward: in his ships there was greater sophistication, better materials and finish. Accommodation for the sailors, though still primitive by land standards, was much improved, and the sawyers and carpenters employed by Ebenezer were skilled at planking, fo'c'sle building, bunk construction and cabinet-making. And they worked reasonable hours, and on Sundays attended chapel with their families.

Ebenezer never forgot that his ships – Porthmadog ships – were to be built at the highest level of craft. Nothing was to be skimped or left to chance. From the heaviest oak timbers – the ribs of the ship – to the smallest brass rivets, everything had to be right. Sometimes after a long hard day, starting at six in the morning, he could be seen as the sun was setting, examining a bucket of nails, transferring them from one bucket to another, looking for the faulty ones, which he could tell by touch.

Before the main quay at Porthmadog had been built (*cei newydd*), shipbuilding took place on the strip of land unfortunately called 'rotten tare'. This piece had been created by ballast from returning ships, dumped on one side of the quay to make the final rectangular shape. On the inner side, an earth bank sloped down to the water which in wet weather became very soft and muddy; this helped in the launching, preventing the scarring of the keel. At the far corner of this piece, the Festiniog Railway claimed pride of place, at *stesion fach* (little station). Originally, there were heavy draft horses to be seen, with their heavy harnesses and black manes. They tugged the carriages back uphill to Blaenau so that slates could be carried, by the strong and often dangerous hand of gravity, back down to the quay. But now, progress had intervened. Steam locomotives ran around the station like ducks on a pond, making puffing and blowing sounds, and piping their whistles.

David Morris had invested in ships before, and made money. This time he had greater confidence and was to own it all himself. He borrowed most of the required sum from the National and Provincial Bank in Lombard Street. He was determined to invest well, build well, hire the best crew, and over the years of sailing make regular profits. One day in the summer of 1867, he placed an envelope containing five hundred pounds in the hand of Ebenezer Roberts. Eben Mawr, as the locals called him, had already started on this new ship, even though he had not been paid anything. He had explored the woods around Tremadog and down towards Beddgelert, marking the required trees with a yellow strip of fabric, hammered to the tree with four nails. He had approached the owner of the land and negotiated a figure per tree. His own men cut the tree and with considerable difficulty rolled the pieces up on to long carts. Stout horses drew them away.

Eben said, "We have the money now. Safe and secure." He closed his hand over the envelope as he said this. "We have the timber. We have the heart of the ship." He was inclined to be rhetorical in his speech.

"But we do not have a name. A ship to have a heart has to have a name."

David Morris stepped closer and looked Eben in the eye. "We shall call her *Excelsior*. Because she will excel. She will be stout. She will be a happy ship."

At this Ebenezer squinted his eyes and turned his head. This touched on something very deep about ships and ship-building. It was widely known that there were happy ships and there were unhappy ships. This started at the beginning, with the gathering of the timber and it went on the whole life of the ship. Call it superstition or whatever, or just common-sense. It was a known fact that sailors wanted to work on a happy ship. And it was not just down to the quality or temper of the ship's master. Sometimes you could have a bad-tempered, incompetent, even drunken captain, and you still had a happy ship. Eben knew that he had a reputation for building happy ships, and he didn't want to lose it.

"*Exelsior*, he said, looking up towards Moel y Gest. "Just as today's sky is blue. Just as it is not too hot or too cold. The timber is gathered. The settings are favourable. She will be a brig. We shall call her *Excelsior* because she will excel."

The money was kept locked in the mahogany cupboard at home, to be banked the next day by the lady of the house. Eben was pleased. His wife cooked beef, his favourite meal, and that night he went to bed early, knowing that tomorrow would be a long and productive day.

Chapter 6

FLORENCE was a year younger than her sister Blanche. They were not as two peas in a pod. They had their distinctive personalities and tastes. Florence was more interested in appearance than Blanche; she chose her clothes with more care and in her room, newly-ironed dresses and skirts hung from the picture-rail to preserve their smooth texture and ironed creases. Blanche was more inclined to throw her pieces in to the tall-boy and the chest with its deep drawers, and sometimes a blouse would lie across a chair for weeks.

Blanche did not fit in easily to the organisation of the household. She was not a conformist. There were complaints about her by members of the household. "Why?" she would assert. "Why all this folding and putting-away. It's just not easy or convenient." The maid would dip away, withdrawing from a confrontation with the sharp-tongued Blanche. There was something quite assertive about Blanche. Physically, she was the more muscular and lean. He shoulders were squarer than her sister's and her brushed-back hair, easily-tied, revealed a forehead and profile more defined than her sister's.

Blanche was ambitious. She wanted to get ahead, to achieve. She had that look in her eyes. Things were to be for her, for her advancement. When it came to company, she was selective. At dinner-parties, she would quickly sort-out the ones worth knowing and the ones not worth knowing. She had been known to look out of the window when a certain widow or heavy-set older man was taking over the conversation, and then to reach for the vegetables in their tureen with a polite request that they should be shared around.

Both girls appreciated the life that they were born into. They had been privately educated and for their age they were unusually articulate. They conducted themselves well. In that way they were similar. But they were different; they saw different qualities in people. Perhaps the ambition and astringency of their father, the local Member of Parliament, had entered their souls, more so in the case of Blanche, who was always thinking "Why?"; "Why should I do this?" "What advantage is it to me?". Her sister was not so self-focussed. She was inclined to take things as they came, and wait for something significant to emerge. We could not say that Blanche had the larger share of wisdom.

This summer morning, they were sitting in the garden. They had decided on a *tête-à-tête*. Every now and then they sat together and tried hard to be relaxed, balanced and objective. They knew that they had to take a rational attitude towards their futures.

They sat on the long white metal chair in the front garden. Each side of them there was tall growth of wood; the road down to the sea, with its neat sandy beach, on their right, past the gable of the tall stone house. The garden before them was sprinkled with flowers. There were two gardeners at Castell Deudraeth, so weeding was regular and thorough. The blue sky was full of round clouds; the slight wind from the sea brushed the tops of the flowers.

Florence lived up to her name. Flowers were her element and her nature. Her complexion was what was called 'peaches and cream'; in this Merionnydd neck of the woods, this quality was rare. Her hair was light brown, with a silkiness that caused it to rise in the breeze, and when the wind was strong it streamed out like a spray of water. She also lived up to her name in regard to the culture of the city of Florence. She was very interested in drawing and had made some attempts at pastel work on an easel set up in the corner of the drawing-room, with its view of Harlech and the Cambrian mountains. There was something visual about

Florence; she was pictorial. Of medium height, she seemed as if she should be in a picture, with her well-proportioned body, bright eyes and mouth that smiled often.

Blanche, on the other hand, was taller, more angular. Her hands were larger and her facial complexion lacked the glow of her sister. Congruent with her friends and neighbours, she was of the darker Welsh sort, her hair almost black, her arms muscular. There was en energy about her. She was not unattractive; she was not pictorial; but she had presence. She had the ability to command. When she raised a hand, the listeners became silent, and her steady and purposive talking was carefully listened-to. At dinner-parties, she was either a great failure or a great success. When her mind was put to it, she was a persuader.

"We must see to it," said Blanche.

"See to what?" replied her sister.

"See to the future," Blanche replied.

It was a mysterious start to a conversation.

"The future is ours," said Blanche. "We must look to it. Put some direction in to it. It won't just happen. We mustn't just wait. Then things could go badly wrong."

She looked across the river Dwyryd.

"The future is like that far bank. That countryside has been created by hand over hundreds of years. Every day somebody has worked on it."

They both saw the pale green fields scattered with sheep and the stone walls between them.

"We must begin to plan. Families don't come out of nothing. We must think about what to do with ourselves."

To Florence this was rather chilling, so deliberate. She had been used to the easy path, going along with the today and letting tomorrow be another time.

"Well, I suppose so," she said in her light voice.

There was a silence.

"You're supposed to take a fancy to someone," said Florence. "But I don't fancy anyone. I have no feelings like that. I see young men and I talk to them but I don't want to be with them, well, not all the time. There are interesting people and there are engaging people, but I am not taken-up. I think you need to be somehow connected, two of you becoming one ..."

"You need to make a team," replied Blanche in her strong tone of voice. "Getting together all round. A group of two with a direction, purpose, ambition. By the time we are thirty, our lives will be half over."

It was a strong thought.

Behind them, their brother was closing the front door. He did it very carefully, without banging. He had his blue striped three-piece suit on with a starched wing collar. He looked every inch the solicitor. He turned to walk to the stables. His black shoes were well polished.

He looked over to his sisters.

"Sorting out the world?" he said, half mockingly.

"Yes," replied the two together.

Arthur Osmond disappeared around the side of the house.

"Made for it," said Blanche. "The eldest son. A busy solicitors' practice. What can be easier? What can go wrong?"

"Things aren't planned for us," said Florence, taking up some of her sister's attitude.

They both became quiet as the sound of a horse's hooves was heard. Arthur Osmond was on his way to work. His grey stallion treaded the back drive, which was on the Porthmadog side. As the fine animal saw the rounded stone gatehouse, he picked-up speed, turned left and trotted comfortably down the main road, then across the new causeway, his head held high in the breeze.

Both girls saw their brother and his conformity as an emblem of the world of work. To have a secure future, they had to make adjustments. They had to try to fit in. How they started to do this was unknown now. They had a future and that future had to be created. Then things would fall in to place.

Chapter 7

THE CARCASS of the *Excelsior* emerged from the earth like the remains of an animal. Huge timbers rose, bending, to the sky. Their tops were uneven, serrated; made of the finest oak. They had been bent through application with steam from exposure to vats of boiling water and they were forced in to place with wooden spars bent against them. The shape of the ship was emerging; the bulge, the height, the shaped keel.

It was dusk in the quay. Workers on ships had departed. Sunlight was fading as two adventurous boys approached the *Excelsior* from different directions. David Williams was coming from the station end, with his back to Penrhyndeudraeth, and David Jones was wandering in from Madog Street from where he had emerged to seek some change from his parents' incessant domesticity. Both boys were in the dusk, half-hidden. They did not see one another.

David Williams had a sharp eye for birds. He could tell them one from another at hundreds of yards. He detested seagulls which were the one kind of flying animal he thought unworthy of that fine act. They were clumsy, ugly creatures. They possessed no grace in the air. Their shape was ungainly and their sound, the worst of all, was horrible.

Both boys, still at school in New Street, knew one another well but were not in the same class. Miss Evans was David Williams's teacher; Mr Hugh Watkins was David Jones's. There was a sturdy presence in both characters, with Miss Evans the more insistent, extending her control to her pupils even to their rhythm of walking as they rose in orderly fashion from their desks. Mr Watkins relied on surprise. One minute he had his hand on your shoulder in sympathy and appreciation, the next minute his whispy moustache was shaking with exasperation.

David Williams had his overcoat on. There was something in his tidy dress and particular way of standing and walking that spoke of control, discipline and a certain determination.

David Jones, on the other hand, was loose and untidy. He was the smaller of the two. He had a swagger in his walk. He wore a peaked cap on the back of his large head. As he looked up over the plankings of the *Excelsior*, he saw the sky gathering and the ungainly shape of a seagull settling on one of the highest timbers.

David Williams picked up a stone. It was a piece of slate, sharp on one side. He held it in his hand for a moment, feeling its weight. He saw the seagull clearly; its large white breast towards him. His hatred of this species rose in him as he put his left foot forward. He pulled back his right arm. He brought it forward and the slate sped from his arm as a projectile. It skimmed through the dusk and he lost sight of it. He saw the seagull raise up, its wings outstretched.

Then came a shout from David Jones. *"Diawl. Diawl. Wedi cael y'n hitio."* (I have been hit). The shout was clear to David Williams's ears and he immediately pulled away. He bent his head down and walked at a fast pace. He knew that running would attract attention. He made his way to the road and crossed the bridge.

David Jones was angry. *"Ryw ddiawl 'nath hwn"* he asserted (some devil has done this). The left sleeve of his jacket was torn. The slate projectile had done its sharp work. Not only had it torn the fabric but it also had torn the skin and flesh. There was a bleeding injury on the side of his left arm. The blood ran over his wrist and down his fingers.

He took the loose piece of his sleeve and wrapped it over the wound. He turned swiftly for home. As he made his way, blood dripped on the uneven ground of the building yard and then on the newly-laid tar of Porthmadog's High Street.

He walked down the lane and came in to his home through the back door. His attempt at covering-up his torn coat and bloody scar was not successful. His mother appeared swiftly around the corner of the stairs. She stopped, her face quickly changing to white; her arms outstretched.

"*Wedi brifo. Fy 'machgen. Yn gwaedu. Sut mae hyn?*" (Injured; my boy; bleeding; how did this happen?)

So there were explanations and protests. And forgiveness. David Jones went to bed that night with a scene imprinted on his mind. A scene of a half-built ship in the darkness with a skimming object flying over it, heading for himself.

Standing close to the wooden construction, he had drawn in, through the dark air, the stone and the blood, some mysterious substance, some essence of commitment and passion, that was to remain with him for ever. His career as a major builder of Porthmadog schooners, the best in the world, was set.

For the rest of his life, there was a scar on his left arm.

Chapter 8

SHON EDWARDS was close to completion. The shape in his head matched the shape in his workroom. He was now at the painting stage. He was fond of green, that glossy green found on fresh moss and lush plants in a greenhouse. He associated it with fertility. It had potential for new growth. It was the colour of the hot jungle, he thought, and he laid it on the lower part – below the two wooden breasts of his carved effigy – with the care of a surgeon. This area had its skirt blowing sideways, the line of the thigh prominent. The hands – you always had to take great care with hands, he thought – were finished, painted in flesh-like colour. The single rose, rising from the right hand, was a vivid crimson. This matched her lips, with their sensuous curve. Her eyes were sea-blue, their azure ovals reminiscent of precious ornamental jewels. Eyebrows were exaggerated. You would be seeing this effigy from below, say from twenty to fifty yards distant. It needs to stand out and you need to recognise it at a glance, and thus know what ship it was attached to.

The following day, the gleaming woman was complete.

In the meantime, his father Tomos had been doing what he was good at, making an utilitarian item out of wood. He chose the best mahogany, beautifully grained. He had built a large long box, with a curved lid that fastened with brass hinges and a hook-and-eye closing. Inside he had attached soft sponges and cotton straps with buckles.

Before the effigy was placed in the box, there was a knock at the door. Shon thought he knew who was there. It was Simon Jones, ship-builder, again.

"*Mae o'n barod,*" (it is ready) he said to the standing figure almost before the door was opened.

"*Tyrd i weld,*" (come and look) he said, this time with a relaxed attitude, quite unlike the last time he had spoken to the buyer of the piece.

Simon stood before the woman in the workroom.

"Well. Well. This is your finest," he said in admiration. His eye followed the depth and curve of the body and the crook of the raised right arm.

"Quite a beauty. She is alive. She is a woman. Who could resist her ..." He was musing. "Perhaps I shall meet her some day. She is ... she has ... the allure." It was a word new to him and this was the first time he had used it. It seemed to embody this figure. It went beyond representation. Simon put out his hand and felt the depth of the thigh. He leaned forward and through his nose he detected not just fresh paint but a sense of far places, exotic sights, jungle creatures and a surviving presence.

"Let's get her out," he announced in his firmest tone. "Let's get her in front of the the people and let's finish the ship." He was a determined, hard-working, man.

"Your final payment," he announced as he pressed a brown envelope in Shon's hand. It contained ten pounds. He handed Shon the accounts sheet which he initialled.

The following Monday was the big day. Then the beautiful box containing the even more beautiful effigy was to be carried by the finest horse and cart the five miles or so from Criccieth to Borth y Gest. It would start at first light, taking the route through Pentrefelin and Wern, coming in to Porthmadog at High Street, then turning up past Terrace Road, up the hill, past William Madocks's house and finally down in to the bay of Borth y Gest. It was to be parked on Simon Jones's ship-building yard beside the towering new ship and the low crag of rock by the road. The box was to be carried up the scaffolding, taken to the prow, opened, the effigy woman raised by the three best carpenters, then attached with brass screws to the ship.

Chapter 9

BORTH Y GEST was proud of its maritime activities. It had grown from a small sea bay on the shores of the Glaslyn/ Dwyryd estuary to a centre for shipbuilding and as a village for retired sea-captains. The two shipyards (sometimes, three) each side of its small bay spoke of its ambition.

'The keel is laid," was an expression suitable for 1868: it was pregnant with growth and future prospects. That the keel was of the *Pride of Wales*, that the owner and entire financier was David Morris and that the designer and builder was the flamboyant and much admired Simon Jones made the inhabitants of Borth y Gest, many of them seagoing folk living up in Ralph Street, very pleased. Simon had said repeatedly that this ship was to be his best. It would have the best timbers, the best fittings and the best decoration, which included Shon's work in the drawings across the stern and in the evocative figurehead.

The narrow ravine of Pen-y-Clogwyn had seen the ship's timbers galloped up them by stout shire horses. The jangling chains of harness, the cracking of whips, the clatter of hoofs, and the encouraging shouts from the horsemen filled the air. The villagers did not mind the dust; they pushed at the carts to urge them up the hill and down in to the bay. Spars and sails, tackle and tanks, ropes and rigging, followed in an endless stream. She was being built stern-out, so her stern pointed towards the distant shore near Harlech. Her high bow rose above the fields of Garreg Wen, where the rock jutted out, subject of the plaintive song of David, his harp and his lost love.

The morning of the launch saw Porthmadog High Street in excitement. David Morris's new ship was to be launched and its figurehead was coming through the street, en-route for Borth y Gest. Crowds gathered to see the powerful horse drawing the box with its brass fittings. It gleamed in the sun like new oil. It needed no help up the hill and when it finally came to a halt in Borth y Gest, flags hung from houses and the curved bay was frilled with bunting. Slogans were written on wooden boards, 'Good luck Pride of Wales'.

Shoring and scaffolding were cleared away so that an uninterrupted view of the ship was available for the first time. Her masts and bowsprit were festooned with gaudy code flags. A silken bargee, thirty feet long, emblazoned with her name, flew from a staff on the main. The elaborate drawings of all sorts of distant plants and animals, of sinuous reptiles in intertwined confusion, which completely covered her stern, were unveiled for the first time. The onlookers, ten deep, were entranced.

She was painted a rich bottle-green, girded with a gold strake. She looked like a new toy in a shop window but two hundred times larger.

The final move was the attaching of the figurehead. In skilled hands, it did not take long. The ship builders, bursting with pride, lined up abreast, passing her from hand to hand. She was hoisted up and held against the bow. Fine quality timber was screwed together to make a platform then fixed to the stout upper timber and the planking below. Shon had provided a base to the figure. This was drilled through and brass screws and nails used to fasten her to the platform. She was very secure. 'This girl', they thought, 'will face anything and will come through'. The effigy's paintwork now was pristine but in the next ten years she was to face the sun and heat of the Indian Ocean. Here the extremes of weather would wear her paintwork, so that her crimson lips faded, the flower in her right hand lose its freshness and her hands turn a silvery-white. Life begins in power and colour, and with travel and time, becomes subdued.

Finally, the launching. It was a moment of some anxiety.

A proper launching makes a good ship. Birth is a major event. A good, easy, uneventful birth is much to be wished.

The young lady stepped forward on the platform.

"Jenny Morris," the onlookers said to each other. "Jenny is to launch the ship." There was excitement and anticipation.

The figurehead was ready. All eyes were on the gleaming new ship with its powerful female emblem. She had her right hand raised, holding a flower.

Jenny smiled. The sunlight caught her golden hair. Now there were two of her, the actual and the representation. She looked at her effigy. There was a flare about Jenny's face, with blue eyes beneath her flowing hair.

She tossed back her head. She said, clearly, "I name this ship *Pride of Wales*."

She brought the bottle up against the timbers with a surprisingly strong move of her right hand. The bottle splintered and the wine ran down the ship's new prow. In front of Tai Pilots, arms were raised and voices rose in enthusiastic chorus.

"Hurrah for *Pride of Wales*. Hurrah for Jenny Morris."

The shipbuilders started to pull, shove and lever. Others joined in on the ropes. The slipway had been well-designed, and heavily greased. She slid, moved downwards, and entered deeper water. She was upright: in magnificent shape.

The enthusiastic cheering continued as the new ship was born and entered her natural element. Jenny looked on in awe and appreciation, at this culmination of thousands of actions by skilled suppliers and builders.

The other side of the Borth y Gest bay, some five hundred yards away, at the point where rocks joined the unkempt grounds of the Spoooner property Bron-y-Garth, two young men stood, looking down at this launching.

They were Charles Edwin Spooner and his elder brother George Percival Spooner ('Percy').

Edwin and Percy had heard the cheering. As they pushed the branches aside, they opened-up the view of Borth y Gest, hung with bunting and streamers. They fastened their eyes on the new ship, Simon Jones's creation, in all its beautiful symmetry

They observed the figurehead erected and fastened in to place.

They saw from a distance a young lady step up to a platform. They saw a yellow glow as her hair caught the sun and they saw the ship slide slowly to the deeper water.

Two men, the figurehead of a woman and a ship.

Little did they know that soon in the future Percy would commit an indiscretion and be posted to the far side of India. And that Edwin, his career in civil engineering prospering, would find himself working on both sides of the Indian Ocean. And that this great ocean was to be crossed, for many years, by the Borth y Gest-built barque *Pride of Wales,* under charter to the Indian Government, carrying state documents and gold.

Chapter 10

TWO WEEKS later at Castell Deudraeth, with a similar sky and the lawn well-trimmed, Florence and Blanche resumed their conversation.

"There's privilege and there's trade. The one you're born in to, the other you work your way in to. We are privileged. We have had our private tutors and our father has worked hard to supply us with good things," said Blanche.

"And of course we appreciate it. But ..." Her eyes turned to the left. "In the village there are people who have to live on one pound a week. Their children go to work and at the end of their lives, they have little to show for it."

Florence had a concerned look about her eyes. "I am inclined to ... drift. I am not a leader. I am a follower. We have been given things, and I might think life will go on like that. Just given things. Fitting in. I will slip in to some space in society. It will be easy."

She was saying what she thought was her character, but she knew that it was also her weakness.

The two girls, well-brought-up, went quiet. They rose separately and drifted back in to the security and warmth of their home.

It was not going to be easy. Life was changing. The old decades were not to move smoothly in to the new decades. The structure of privilege was dissolving.

Around them up in the hills of Blaenau Festiniog and down there near the seashore where new ships were being made, trade was working hard, from early morning until night-time. New money was being made. Old money was thinning out. Energy, power, ambition; all of this was in slate, in the railways and new ships; in production and distribution.

Their father, David Williams, barrister-at-law, Liberal MP for Merioneth, was not one for perpetuating the past, for profit was in embracing the present and being an essential part of it. He worked hard and he made sure that he was known as an agency of progress.

On the fifteenth of December 1869, their father died.

The funeral cortege, a long black line, stretched almost all the way from the new embankment, now known as 'the cob', to the opening of the Castell Deudraeth drive in Minffordd.

Chapter 11

THE VIEW; the grandeur. The Spooner family acquired space as they acquired ambition. They had vision.

The grandfather, James Spooner, took the lease to William Madocks's house, Tanyrallt, in Tremadog. Here Madocks, as the eighteenth century turned in to the next, had looked over his estate, over the one long embankment that pushed the sea back and over the second embankment which brought slate down on rails from Blaenau Ffestiniog. This vision was the lode-stone of the development of Porthmadog as the centre of trade and employment.

The sea was always the inspirer. It allowed for expanse, for exchange, for growth. Carriage by sea was expected and fulfilling. Slate was heavy; water was light. Floating was easier than dragging. Where there was opportunity and necessity, men assuaged the sea and made their sweat work with it. They raised masts towards the skies. The stuff of sail rose and billowed and allowed the free air to profit from it.

In 1834 James Spooner and his family moved to live in Morfa Lodge, where the vision – the view – continued, again through the eyes of Madocks who had built the house, but died in 1828.

In 1830 came the crucial event: Henry Archer commissioned James Spooner to survey a suitable route for the Festiniog Railway. Here, it was determined, was the vein along which the wealth would flow; slate-wealth.

James Spooner's son, Charles, inherited the role at the railway and the vision. He, in the 1850s, moved with his family to Tu hwnt i'r bwlch, a large stone house again at the back of Porthmadog, again linked inexorably with the growing of the port and its business. The house was a twin of Morfa Lodge, both built next to one another and looking regally down on the port and its activities. It had been built and occupied by John Williams, Madocks's agent and again it symbolised progress, and some completion, of the great scheme. Success and profitability flowed down the new rails from the great slate quarries of Blaenau Ffestiniog to Porthmadog. It extended across the new quays and travelled thousands of miles in export of slate in hand-built ships, to far lands. Without the sea, and sailing-ships, none of this would have happened.

Charles Easton then moved with his family to the high-set Bron-y-Garth, Borth y Gest, where out of the top large sash windows he could see the ever-changing tides negotiating the sands of the estuary and the schooners cutting their ways through the changing channels of the combined rivers Dwyryd and Glaslyn.

So, two Spooners, father and son. But what of the next generation?

One stood out. George Percival. 'Percy'. He had been admired that day in the garden of Bron-y-Garth by the sisters Blanche and Florence Williams. He had the training; he had the ability; he had the presence.

Educated at Harrow; trained in engineering at Karlsruhe Polytechnic; apprenticed through his father at the Festiniog Railway at Boston Lodge, its HQ on the Merioneth side of the cob, he was set for a glittering career. His confidence was high. His prospects – his vision – was laid out before him. Profits from the railway were good and Bron-y-Garth prospered.

There is no doubt that in the engineering works, full of men with real talent, George Percival, the boss's son, was highly respected. With his sleeves rolled-up, the steel ruler in his right hand, sitting on a stool at the large sloping-top oak desk, the shapes he created, his men knew, would work.

He instinctively knew what would translate in to metal. His foreman lifted his page of drawings off the desk with a swirl of confidence. It was pored over in silence by men who had the dark grey of iron-dust in their skin.

The new locomotive *James Spooner*, named after his grandfather, took shape with determined but unaffected ease of engineering. This design was improved to create *Livingston Thompson*, a very fine locomotive. Bogie frames, carriages and guards vans flowed from his pen in the 1870s. On the drawing-board, he did not put a foot wrong.

But Percy was destined for a very different future, in a very different place.

Chapter 12

Fynnon Sam Richards sat at the foot of the cliffs at the entrance to Porthmadog harbour. There were four quays here and ships habitually moored by them. Water from this well was used to fill casks and tanks, thus saving the halfpenny per gallon tax raised by the Port Authorities on ships re-filling at the central quays.

In the early evening, the cross-piece of the well could be seen turning. The water barrel came up and the silver water flowed out of it in to the metal tank held by three sailors. The evening was quiet except for the shouts of the water-fetchers – *"Iawn." "Ara deg. Ara deg." "Llawn"*. The tank had a rail around it. Now the three sailors grasped it and hoisted the tank, carrying it towards their schooner.

Jenny was used to this. Often she had gazed down to the busy port from Y Garth which was the name given to this elevated section of road and residences that loomed up behind the harbour on the top road to Borth y Gest.

She had frequently walked along Clogwyn-y-Pig, a lane which started at Marine Terrace, ran along the cliff side, finishing at Borth y Gest's Trwyn Cae Iago. It presented a marvellous panorama of the blue hills of Ardudwy and the great estuary expanse of the Dwyryd and Glaslyn , with its vibrant and ever-changing moods.

It was a lane for lovers and farewells. Many a young man in his ship, destined for the unknown, had last seen his young woman waving at him from the Clogwyn, her arm fading as the ship moved away.

Over this lane was the rock known as 'The Pig'. It jutted out rather like the bowsprit of a ship. And on this was, secured by iron bolts, was a large wooden goat. To creep cautiously out and sit astride the goat was the dare-devil delight of the boys of the district. They would stand on the goat, risking their lives. This goat marked the harbour. Returning sailors would raise a tired hand to it: it was a talisman of welcome and safety.

This rock was blasted away when space for the quay entrance was needed. It rock went in to the foundations of the new quays. A new lower road was created, known as Lon Cei, which was no substitute in beauty for the old Ffordd Clogwyn-y-Pig.

Jenny was well used to changes. All around her, things were happening at speed. She had smashed the bottle against the polished bulk of *Pride of Wales*, seen the pristine ship ease herself in to the water of the estuary. Around her was the detritus of shipbuilding, the tall bending spars, the piles of frayed rope, pieces of wood and canvas, the greased cradle through which the ship slid down to the water. This was her place; these pieces were the necessary aspect of work and creation. Ships were her new life.

Her new young man was a ship man – a sailor through and through. From a small-farming family, as most of them were, he was muscular, medium-height, with brown eyes and well-tanned skin. William Hughes was a sailing man from the beginning and on the *Excelsior* he knew the ropes. He was entirely reliable and capable and even though still a young man he had the calm capability of an experienced sailor.

They conversed in Welsh.

"Everywhere, all over, all around us, there is life and work," she murmered as she looked over the new town and harbour from Clogwyn-y-Pig. She held his hand. It was firm. She kissed it slowly and deliberately.

His brown eyes were part of the kaleidoscope of the port and sailing. Masts and spars crossed the lower sky. Their sway in the wind was as the winding-up of energy before the long trip.

"It is my way," he said. "It is something I can do. I understand ships. I understand the ocean." His voice was quiet but firm.

They were married in 1871 when she was only twenty years old.

Chapter 13

THE BRIG *Excelsior* had two masts equipped with spars holding four square sails and a boom to the rear for a fore-and- aft sail. Built in 1868, she was a sea-roamer; of registered tonnage of one hundred and seventy-six, she could carry 300 tons of dead weight cargo. She was a sturdy carrier; she shifted many thousands of tons of phosphate rock from the Spanish main and the Dutch Antillies to Europe. She was built of Welsh oak and she plied her trade in the Atlantic for over twenty-five years.

In 1871, with the two honeymooners on board, they sailed from Antwerp to Villanueva in the Province of Barcelona. But Jenny was no sailor; she was frequently sea-sick. Their accommodation was poor – a small fo'castle, low down in the fore peak, and a mahogany-panelled cabin to the rear. Living space was confined and stuffy, with living quarters often sealed to keep out the wind and rain. The deck was often awash and this boat had a terrier-like shake when faced with heavy seas.

At Villanueva, the high mountains of the Catalonia range formed a backdrop. The weather had improved, the wind died, and the hot sun of the Mediterranean shone down. In the foreground were vinyards and farm houses. There were fruit stalls in the harbour, cobbled streets with carts carrying wine in baskets, drawn by horses. It was quaint and very much a contrast with Caernarfonshire.

They were welcomed by the wife of the British Consul. In her cream house on the hillside, she poured tea for her guests.

"A long and difficult voyage," she said, evoking sympathy.

"But you are very welcome here. Have you brought salt cod?" she asked.

"Not this time," replied William, setting the tone of an experienced mariner. "But we have a busy trade with Spain, Portugal and Greece. We are on the coast of Spain often. Many ships from Porthmadog have carried salt cod across the Atlantic. It is a well-known thing. The Catholic countries need it for their Friday food."

"Indeed," she replied. "And I believe that when the Spaniards and Italians go across the Atlantic to settle in the new Americas, the sailing ships carrying salt cod follow them, and so the business expands.

"And what are you carrying?" she questioned.

William replied, "We are bound for Sicily. There is sulphur there and we shall be carrying it back."

"I hear the place is most unpleasant," she said, and she was right.

They departed the house as if moving away from civilisation. It had smooth paintwork, sash windows and secure wrought-iron railings. They turned towards their primitive ship, and the unsteady ocean.

When the *Excelsior* pulled in to the harbour at Girgenti, it was as if the whole area had been painted with a pale yellow colour. It covered the ships in the harbour and the harbour buildings. The ship's sails were stained a patchy yellow, resembling a used hankerchief.

The stuff was loaded. Jenny was sitting on the cabin settee when she heard a shout and there was a commotion on deck. The cabin door was flung open and a large wet cloth was thrown over her head. Her arm was grasped and she found herself hanging over the ship's edge. There was a fire on board and danger of suffocation. Eventually the fire was extinguished but the living quarters held a foul smell for days.

After a delay in Gibraltar, the voyage back home began. But the Bay of Biscay was in one of its defiant moods. At the height of a storm, three sailors were given an important job on the main lower-top-sail yard. It was perilous. The three men clung to one another. One of them moved to get a better purchase but slipped and fell in to the sea. He was never seen again. It was an event which never left her. It remained as a reminder of the exceptional dangers sailors faced when they went abroad in sailing ships.

Jenny heard the wonderful words "White cliffs" and soon was planning her exit from the vessel. But the bad seas held and the coastguard station at Deal said that the Captain and his wife would be met at Deal Pier. The long-boat was launched, a fourteen-foot clinker-built open boat manned by four sailors. Jenny, not one to complain, was hoist from this to the pier, lashed to a rope.

All this was a contrast to the day she had spent in Borth y Gest, standing proudly on a platform, launching the *Pride of Wales*, which was an elegant, long, ship, built by a craftsman designer, belonging to a new generation of vessels; very different from the sturdy but juddery *Excelsior*.

Jenny had not enjoyed her honeymoon. The voyage was long, the conditions cramped and stifling. She later recalled a story where an old sailor had been 140 days at sea. On his way to a main line station in London, he saw a street vendor with a cage of chaffinches. "How much are they each?" he enquired. "Two and six pence," the hawker replied. "How many are there?" asked the sailor. "Fifteen," came the reply. "I'll have the lot," the sailor replied. He handed over his hard-earned money, taking the cage and opening its door. The birds flew out of the cage and in to freedom, and the happy sailor made his way home.

Chapter 14

IN FEBRUARY of 1871 there was an important gathering at the Festiniog Railway. It was Charles Easton Spooner's big event. He and Mr Livingston Thompson (Managing Director) were the hosts. The world of narrow-gauge railways came to them. Spooner had commissioned Robert Francis Fairlie to design and build a locomotive which they named *Little Wonder*. It was a little wonder because it behaved with great spirit on the narrow, twisting, steep line that went up to Blaenau Ffestiniog and back. It was an articulated double-engine locomotive, ideally suited to this type of line.

The trials were more successful than they hoped. Russian observers were present. Also two observers from the Denver and Rio Grande Railroad. Lt Gen. Sir William Baker and others from the India Office also attended.

Arthur Osmond Williams of Castell Deudraeth, young local solicitor and trustee of the Madocks estate, was there. He saw the gleaming double-Fairlie and made the right noises.

"Much success," he said, turning to Charles Spooner. "The design is right. Fairlie has good ideas, though I am told that Percy and Willliam Williams had a hand in the design, with some modifications."

Charles was a fair man, and agreed. "William Williams realised that a single boiler would not do so he designed two, one at each side. Percy drew it up. And the result is a more powerful locomotive than we expected. Although space for the second man on the footplate is very tight."

The Little Wonder set off on another trip up to Blaenau, this time hauling twenty carriages and wagons. It hooted regularly as it went over the cob.

"Hoot. Hoot," said Blanche as she watched it depart. "Look at all these men."

A knot of men surrounded Fairlie, who was taking in the praise. One of them was a young solicitor, Percival Currey. He was in a similar position to young Arthur Osmond, the eldest son of a local solicitor, but he was from Kent. The Currey firm had handled some of Fairlie's business and it was important that they had an observer at this important trialling of one of Fairlie's major designs. Fairlie can be said to be a self-publicist and at times he got carried away with his own importance. You would think from his manner that he had invented the locomotive and that all the world's railways were created by him. So he needed watching in case he promised something or gave something away which was not to his commercial advantage. Percival's father has realised that Fairlie needed control and guidance from the time they met in a London club. Here in this surprisingly pleasant day in the corner of Caernarfonshire, an important step forward in the development of railways, especially narrow-gauge ones, was taking place, and this little engine, with it double body and vigorous presence, was chuffing away as if the future was being created by its confident self.

Olaf from Denver was especially impressed. His American drawl dominated the proceedings. He had a habit of shouting "Good Man. Good Man. Keep it going. Good Man" as the engine showed its mettle. He had a special relationship with locomotives and regarded them as practically members of the human race.

Blanche moved closer to the group of men around Fairlie. She saw that Currey had placed himself close to his employer, placing his shoulder against anybody who seemed to be getting too close. He did not want any of the group to go away thinking that they had got Fairlie to promise to anything.

"And then ..." she heard Currey say "... we have licences. There are three different ones, all drafted by our firm, with my father overseeing. There is the double-Fairlie itself, exclusive rights to build and use, within a given territory. Then, whole country rights, which would be more expensive. And then there would be wide territory rights, such as the whole of South America, the most expensive. But this design is unique. It will draw more freight for its size and fuel than any present engine. It will be efficient and it will make larger profits." In all of this, the contribution of William Williams in turning the design from a promising one to a highly successful one was forgotten, as was many a talented man's contribution from the employed class to the income and reputation of his employer.

Blanche looked at Percival Currey. She was reminded of her brother: the same long face and sharp jaw. Long hair, well-combed. Tall physique, muscular, lithe. His gesticulating hands had a presence, splitting the space between Fairlie and his admirers. He was a man at the beginning of a successful career; he had the advantages of good birth and education, and yet was a seasoned practitioner in the real world of contracts, deals and competition which was the world they were all now engaged in.

Charles Eason Spooner, naturally, was a prominent member of the group around Fairlie. He had approached the great man, commissioned a design from him, which was built and in future the design would be built at the Porthmadog Boston Lodge locomotive works.

"Blanche, my dear," said Charles as he stepped out of the group. "Let me introduce you."

"Our dear friend, Robert Fairlie." Robert F. stepped forward in a flourish, shaking her vigorously by the hand as his gold watch-chain rattled contentedly.

"And his lawyer and adviser, Percival Currey."

Percival stood closely before her. He stooped. He took both her hands in his.

"Great pleasure," he said in his clear south London tones.

"And an enthusiast for railways?"

"It is the way of the future. We have to get used to such things," she replied with a degree of caution.

"We do indeed."

The two of them had now become detached from the Fairlie group. Currey was turning his attention to the attractive Blanche Williams.

There was a congruency between them.

"You are a railway person?" he enquired.

"Not really. Although the line of the Festiniog Railway passes a few hundred yards from our house. Over there." She pointed to the headland that separated the Glaslyn and Dwyryd rivers.

"You hear it in the morning?" he said.

"Yes, about seven thirty. It peeps away as it carries men and machinery to the slate quarries up at Blaenau Ffestiniog."

"Blaenau Ffestiniog," he repeated. "What a fine name. I must learn to pronounce it properly."

"You must learn Welsh," she laughed.

"Perhaps you will teach me," he replied.

Chapter 15

IOAN MADOG and Gwilym Eryri were two men who wrote poetry in Welsh. They were friends; they were peers; they were men of the wind and sea. One was a blacksmith; the other was a sail-maker.

Both worked hard. They were at their work on the quay in Porthmadog shortly after six in the morning. Around them were the myriad trades and craft pieces connected with ship-building. They both contributed to this trade.

Ioan Madog was his bardic name – John of Porthmadog. His real name was John Williams. There were so many Williamses working around the quayside and on the railway in Porthmadog that a foreigner to the area might well believe that it was all a family business.

He had come from iron-working stock. His father, Richard Williams, was the blacksmith at the original Tremadog, when William Alexander Madocks decided that one man from each trade should work in the ideal community, and have his family's accommodation secured. Even today, the sash windows of houses in Tremadog have their frames secured by a brass fastener of exquisite design, manufactured by, or from a design by, the local blacksmith Richard Williams and his son.

John's relatives worked on the Festiniog Railway. Their genius with metal built turntables, carriages, wheels, engines and suchlike. When a problem arose in braking, as it does between a metal set of wheels and iron rails, John Williams was called to solve the problem. He designed a sandbox so that when the train was descending it dropped sand on the rails to give purchase to the wheels when the brake was applied.

But his *piece-de-resistance* was his windlass. Set on board a ship, with its top rim of polished brass and its curving mahogany body, it took a rope to itself and gave enough slack and enough tautness to keep the ship in position at anchor. It could be worked by one man. When there was a light breeze in the harbour, the clicking of the cogs in the windlasses could be heard, similar to the sounds of clocks in a clockmaker's workshop.

John was creative. He made beautiful brass hinges. On a long voyage, these hinges were admired by sailors and many a time his name was mentioned when a Porthmadog ship was anchored at the Azores or off Buenos Aires.

Similarly with Gwilym Eryri, also known as William Roberts, sailmaker. From his loft in the early morning, he was as if on a ship, high in the air. He looked down on the quayside, saw the trades, the business of ship-building as it progressed through the day. He saw the carrying of wood, the chopping, steaming and setting, the oak spurs curving upwards; the carpenters in their aprons with adze and plane; he saw the deck take shape, the masts lifted up and secured and the sails in mounds of white carried on board and finally attached to masts and spars with brass fittings.

He loved sails. The colour of snow, the fabric fascinated him. It was not white, but many colours. The colour picked up the colour of its environment, as a mirror reflects its surroundings. It goes from grey to pink to blue, sometimes dazzling, sometimes subdued and absorbing. Laid across the long wooden floor of his loft, when nobody else was there, he would walk to the middle of the stretch of canvas and laid himself down on it, arms wide, face down, absorbing its texture and smell. It was as if he was in the middle of the best countryside, full of grass, fine trees, flowers and a long view. It had odour. Of flowers in a wood, of the small fields on the slopes of Moel-y-Gest. As the material was being sewn, he would put his fingers around the sewn edge and feel the texture of the fabric. When he felt it, he could tell what it was made of and which supplier he had bought it from. He lived by his senses and in his loft over the harbour in newly-created Porthmadog, he was in his element.

Two men. Tradesmen. Fastened to their skill. And both, bending over their paper with pen in hand, creating the intricate sounds of *cynghanedd,* that strict-metre form of poetry which goes back to the court poets of the Middle Ages. When they had written a few lines, they would recite them, hearing the music embedded in the echoing and rhyming, creating a sound which combined the sounds of nature with the meanings embedded in words. To create cynghanedd you need a very full vocabulary, which they both possessed because as children they had parents who prided themselves in the richness of their Welsh.

Chapter 16

It WAS a love affair. It was sanguine. It stretched through the day as a necessity but also easily, without strain. He came up from Kent and arrived by carriage at Castell Deudraeth, she waiting through the afternoon, eager to hear the sound of wheels on the gravel and then the heavy breathing and snorting of the two horses. A well-cut pair of black shoes, the modern suit, the strong hands, the swerve in the hair, it was as she had imagined and expected. He smiled. She raised her arms. He swung himself against her in a light joyousness.

"It has been sunshine," he announced, not quite truthfully but fully expressive of his mood.

"Let's go and talk with mother," announced Blanche. "I think she is in the kitchen."

Over the deal table, warmed by the iron range, Blanche took hold of the conversation. "Mother," she said. "This is my good friend Percival. He has come up for a few days."

"Indeed. And you are very welcome, Mister Currey."

"Percy, please."

"The blue bedroom shall be yours," she replied with a smile. "With the squirrels and the rooks in the trees. We shall try to make you feel at home."

This was not an empty comment. Annie Louisa had done a little research on the Currey family and found them well established in a leafy corner of north Kent, well situated for daily travel to the City of London, where the family law business was situated.

"Margaret," she said, turning to the maid. "Please prepare the blue bedroom. And ask Henry to take up Mr Currey's valise."

Sitting on the couch in the drawing room that evening, Percy's hand was seen to engage with Blanche's. Both looked radiantly happy. It was as if all was set for them. The evening was balmy. They stepped outside to enjoy the air. The trees had a deep blue tint and below them the river Dwyryd flowed to the sea.

"Wonderful place," he said with honesty. "Such a fine place to grow up in."

"Yes. Thanks to Father. We all miss him. Such a loss. I would have liked him to meet you. You and father would have had so much to talk about: the business, the changes, the need for recording, for honesty of dealing. Such a lot."

"Tradition," he replied. "That is what we have. We have hundreds of clients, some very large ones, and they rely on us to see their paper-work done properly. Sometimes, lives, fortunes, depend on us. The responsibility is sometimes heavy."

She had not expected this earnestness. And yet she knew that this young man had knowledge and understanding. He was rounding out to be her ideal. He was, as many young men are to their loving young women, the image of her father.

"Change is the world we are in now," she said. "The old settled ways are going. Down there on the Dwyryd, a famly of people called Philistine owned barges and they took slates from near Maentwrog, over there, down to the sea, off Garreg Wen, where the slates were hoisted on to sea-going ships. Then the cob was built, then the railway, and now slates are on the quayside and the ships anchor there to take them to all parts of the world. And the Philistines, I'm sorry to say, went completely out of business.'"

"How fascinating," he said. "These slate-carrying ships, where do they come from?"

"We make them," she said, proudly. "By hand. On this shore. On these beaches."

"Fantasic," he said. "It an integrated business. Manufacture, use, investment, insurance, profits, all together. The best sort."

"Yes, and ordinary people own them. They buy a sixty-fourth of a trading vessel. Shopkeepers, farmers and teachers, they all invest in our industry."

"I would love to see some of this," he said.

She replied, "Tomorrow, we'll ride over to Borth y Gest. A ship is being built there now."

They turned back towards the house as the trees settled down and the sky darkened.

The next morning they were mounted on two mares and were trotting gently in the direction of Borth y Gest. They passed over the cob, trod carefully among the goods set for ship-building, turned up the hill past Morfa Lodge, the large house Madocks built for his new family, which he did not survive to live in, and before them was an opening with the sea in the distance. They saw wooden uprights peeping above the ridge of Trwyn Cae Iago and as they turned the corner, the ship-building came fully in focus.

Both horses were drawn up together. They dismounted. A man in an apron with white hair approached.

"What is this ship?" asked Blanche.

"She is *The Fleetwing* ma'am" he replied. "We are finishing her decking now."

"Who is her builder?" she enquired.

"Richard Jones of Garreg Wen," he replied. "Here he is now."

They were approached by a man of medium stature with a mop of dark hair. Under his arm he carried rolls of paper.

He touched his hat, "Ma'am."

"And you are the builder?"

"Yes, and designer."

"All this, you are responsible for?"

"Yes. But I have the best help. The best men. These men could build a ship blindfold." He laughed

"And the finance?" asked Percival.

"All arranged through an office in Porthmadog. Shareholdings all by Pritchard Brothers. And insurance arranged locally. We are all part of a local business."

"Where will she sail?" asked Percival.

"She can sail the world," replied Richard. "She is strong and she will cut through the largest wave."

"Where did you study to be a designer and shipbuilder?" asked Percival.

"Over there," replied Richard, pointing to the rock known as Y Garreg Wen. "I used to sit on that rock and watch the schooners sail the estuary, in and out. I used to make sketches on paper. They were my toys. My parents are small farmers at Garreg Wen. They can not read or write. But they are honest people."

"Amazing," said Percival.

He reached forward and shook Richard's hand with a sense of genuine humility and respect.

"Back to work," said Richard cheerfully.

They watched the back of his black waistcoat disappear in the mix of builders, scaffolding and timber.

Chapter 17

BLANCHE WINEFRED Wynn Williams (born 1855) was married to Percival Currey (born Lewisham,Kent, 1851) in 1875.

Blanche did not want to leave her native soil. She had grown up here, developed her ideas here. The view from the drawing room of Castell Deudraeth was as if engraved on the front of her mind.

But it was the convention. A woman marries a man and the woman lives with him in the area where he has his business. She becomes his support, his helper, his other half; she is with him when times are good and when times are bad. She knew that. But she was resentful that she had to leave. She had grown up where the Dwyryd and the Glaslyn met; with views of Cnicht and the Moelwyns; the harbour at Porthmadog and its miniature in Borth y Gest; and the sometimes threatening darkness of the long view over the breakwater out to the Irish Sea.

But before they were married, an idea came up which modified that, making it easier for her to leave. It came from that day the year before when they drew up their horses and saw the *Fleetwing* being built. The idea was grounded in the sturdiness of that ship, built with the skill of local men. It represented locality, the here-and-now, the home and hearth. It represented the people she had grown up with.

"We shall have a ship built. It will be your representative here. So you still belong here."

This statement was made by Percival.

Somehow he had understood the problem. The problem which lay deep in his future wife's mind and heart.

She responded with pleasure and awe.

And so it was in the winter of 1874/5 that the two of them rode their horses through Porthmadog, taking the Morfa Bychan road. They went past the turning to Borth y Gest. They descended towards the long bow of the seashore, turning left in to a lane. They trotted through thick trees and turned to the right, stopping by a simple farmhouse with small casement windows and front door with a surprisingly elaborate brass knocker.

They saw the bunch of hair first, but this time he had no rolls of paper under his arm. He had a wide, boyish, smile for them. He had remembered.

"How is the *Fleetwing*?" asked Percival.

"A1 at Lloyds" was the businesslike answer. "Flying across the oceans like an albatross. We built her strong and safe and that's what she is."

"How would you like to build another ship? For us," asked Percival in his calmest manner, moving his left hand towards Blanche.

Richard went quiet and then a huge wave of pleasure washed over his face. He loved the sea and he loved carpentry. He loved the tension between the two. He wanted the wind to blow its full force and he wanted his ship to square up to it.

"What pleasure. A new one. Just when I was thinking that things were going slack."

They were sitting in his front room. The china dogs sat each side of the mantelpiece and between them four lustre jugs. His parents had moved to the back kitchen. Richard leaned forward and thrust the poker in to the fire.

"What do you have in mind?"

Percival replied, "Something very much part of the business of the area. She should make regular trips and be in Porthmadog a good time for all to see. She will have a presence in the harbour and be seen as a reliable vessel. She will stand for Blanche and how her family have a heritage and presence here."

Richard asserted, "Useful, manoeuverable. An effective

carrier, making good business. At the moment phosphate from the West Indies is a regular and profitable trade. Just over one hundred feet long, with a depth of say thirteen feet; a brig, two masts square-rigged. Very practical." Richard was already visualising the ship in his mind.

"And she will be beautiful."

Percival became insistent, "Blanche and I will not take a public position on this ship. We will let her emerge as the others have. By public subscription, by local banking and insurance; by shares owned by local people. We want her to be a solid product of the ship-building industry here and we want her to be owned by local people who will profit by their investment," he said, laying down the policy and philosophy. "Above all, I want her to be as Blanche is ..." he asserted with a glance at his future wife.

The group paused. The fire popped and hissed as a small smouldering log fell down.

"You will need a ship's husband," said Richard.

"A ship's husband," retorted Blanche. "What on earth is that?"

"They are essential to this business," replied Richard. "They are the practical people who make it all work. The shareholders need them to pay all the expenses of the ship, such as buying stores, paying the sailors, and so on."

"Whom shall we have?" asked Percival.

"I suggest Prichard Brothers," said Richard. "They are well established and respected. And they employ very good bookkeepers."

I shall contact them," said Percival. "And I shall have a word with Thomas Casson; I am sure he will see things well ordered."

He continued, "But, and I want you to understand: I am behind the venture. I will ensure there are no practical impediments. The ship will go ahead immediately. For that end, I wish you to accept this." He reached in his pocket and removed a wad of paper money. "Two hundred pounds for now."

He handed the money to Richard.

Richard got out of his chair, moved to the desk in the corner and wrote out a receipt.

"And I shall be proud to be a shareholder," said Richard, wearing his wide smile.

They rose to leave.

And what shall we call her?" asked Richard.

"We shall call her *Blanche Currey*, Percival replied confidently.

Blanche looked stunned.

They shook hands.

The planked front door clicked behind them.

They directed their horses back to the main road and up the hill towards Porthmadog. But they could not resist turning right for Borth y Gest. They stopped at the point they had stopped at before, when they looked at the building of the *Fleetwing*.

Percival said, "Here, we shall have a ship. It is a birth. It will in a sense be part of our family." The sea was flowing and it lapped over the rocky shore below the headland Trwyn Cae Iago, on the Porthmadog side of the the small bay at Borth y Gest.

Blanche was overwhelmed. "I am thrilled. A whole ship. My, what a gift. Let it flourish."

Two days later, early in the morning, six men were to be seen at this spot handling long wooden spars. They fastened them to the ground securely and started building a cradle, a basket-like structure within which the ship was to be built.

Passers-by looked in their direction and the inevitable questioning started. Richard Jones, Garreg Wen, has a new commission. What is it? Who will run and own it? What is she called?

On the matter of names, the name of the ship did not strike public consciousness for a month or two. By this time Blanche was planning her marriage in Kent and the ship taking shape on the sands of Borth y Gest was her representative, her token of presence in memory, on this shore of Caernarfonshire.

Chapter 18

DAVID JONES, shipbuilder of Porthmadog, was vigour personified; a ship-builder *par excellence*. He was not a social figure. He preferred the anonymity of the boatyard. He was one of 'the men' and he never pretended to be anything else. When his prominent boatyard on the harbour – '*cei newydd*' – was approached by one intent on doing business with him, selling him spars, ropes or nails, or even the intention of a new ship, David Jones would be in the centre of the group of working men, looking like them, thinking of his next physical task.

However, it is a fact that he built more, and better, ships here than anyone else, apart from his later rival, who was now at sea, David Williams.

And the *C.E.Spooner* had his stamp all over it.

It was to be a barquentine; three-masted, with all but the foremast fore-and-aft rigged. Five square sails hung from her foremast. The rig was developed for the trade: slates carried to Hamburg, then general cargo to Cadiz; salt to Newfoundland and cod back to Mediterranean countries. She had over four thousand square feet of sail.

Sail was the engine. It battled the seas. It expanded with pneumatic energy, taking the wind and carrying it in a bowl of purpose. It had noise, it had music. Sometimes a sailor would put his ear to the canvas and say that he had heard the weather coming, and the sails would be adjusted accordingly. Fore-and-aft sails were the serious carriers, collecting moving air, exaggerating it, collecting it repeatedly for the ocean voyage; purposive and deliberate.

The C.E.Spooner was the finest of its type; it carried its enormous sails with confidence. Above the harbour, in Garth Cottage, the three masts of this ship were observed with close interest; they were pin-sharp in the air.

Mrs Jones of Garth Cottage had her face to the window. She was the *Spooner's* 'ship's husband'. Mrs Catherine Jones had proved her ability through working for a local bank and for local solicitors. For ten years she had performed all the required bookkeeping tasks, seen the investment money come and go, until the day she decided to take on the task of administrating a ship on her own. It was as if she was starting a family and the Spooner was her baby. She looked down at her in the harbour with the look of a mother observing her child. She had a clear view of the activities at David Jones's boatyard.

When she handled a bill from a sailmaker, which included tarpaulins, for £200, she made sure, by looking down at the shore with her sharp eyes, that all the required sails, of the right dimensions, were included and delivered.

She had a small boy, her brother's son, who was not too keen on school, running errands for her, down to David Jones's yard and up again to Garth; he ran up and down, leaping the slate steps, with a paper in his hand, as if it was the finest thing in the world.

As she stepped out of her house one morning, she observed the figure of Charles Easton Spooner coming towards her.

"Good morning," she said.

"Very fine. Very fine." He replied with a raise of his hat.

"And are you looking after my ship?" he asked with a smile.

"Very much so. All is in order. I am doing it all myself, and I can account for every nail, every yard of canvas. I know down to the last minute how much time it is taking to build her."

"Excellent," he replied. "There is no-one better. A single person in charge is better than a group. A single person knows all the details and there is no arguing about where the papers are and what the accounts mean. Please make sure that all the manifest is explained in full."

Charles was speaking from experience. He had driven the Festiniog Railway forward with the force of his personality and his efficiency with paper-work.

"If it can be done directly, face-to-face, and you have a good team, it always works out better. The danger comes when you send messages on paper or via somebody else; then things frequently go wrong."

Catherine agreed, "Yes. And I think David Jones is of the same mind. Your ship – can I call her that? – is coming along very well. I have spoken to him and he has agreed to all the details. Captain Robert Jones of Cae Ednyfed, Minffordd, has accepted the Captainship."

"Two officers, one of whom is a Master Mariner, and four hands. Six is enough," said Charles Easton, with his usual eye on economy.

"And she is a barquentine. That means that she has a foremast of square sails and two other masts with fore-and-aft sails. So she will need less handling on board; the more sails, the more men you need to handle them," replied Catherine, her knowledge of shipping on display.

"How the sails are is how she will behave on the sea. Skilled sailors will make adjustments. Every change of the wind needs a new setting of sail," continued Catherine.

"I would like to feel that the hands are properly housed. Good bunks, that sort of thing ... And let her have a good steward; keep the hands well fed," said Charles.

"I will look to that," replied Catherine.

"I will step forward. The Festiniog Railway awaits me."

Charles Easton touched his hat and proceeded down the hill. At the bottom, he turned sharp right and proceeded past the pub called The Ship to the harbour. He walked along beside the huge granite stones of the harbour walls, turning over the bridge, making for the Festiniog Railway station, where metal working and technology awaited him.

Chapter 19

IOAN MADOG had died. The day of his funeral co-incided with the launch of the *C.E.Spooner.*

Porthmadog's quay was scattered with men and women dressed in their best black. Sunday clothes were evident. Some women wore black veils over their faces, in the way of their grandmothers. The men wore bowler hats, their waistcoats decorated with gold chains, their black boots well polished.

Two black stallions had been carefully selected for their good temper. The coffin was unusually elegant. It had been made by John Willliams's brother Richard – called 'Beuno' – another blacksmith who had a workshop on the '*cei*' (harbour). The quay was in mourning. John Williams was a much respected man, not only for his skill in metal but for his dedication to religion and to his craft of poetry. He came from a long line of poets who were scattered across Meirionnydd. He had been photographed by John Thomas, the travelling photographer, who had caught him in a sober mood, long-faced and steady. And he was an inventor. His design for a windlass had not been patented and was said to have been widely copied by ship-owners on both sides of the Atlantic. Boston harbour, USA, it was said, contained ships featuring the John Williams windlass.

The coffin cart with its four large wheels moved forward in parallel with the flowing seawater. The two stallions paused on the quayside as the nearby ship swayed in the wind, its three masts cutting across the sky. It had a bold, strong bowsprit. On it two workmen stood, caps in hand. The other workmen stood to the fore on the deck, each side of the bow, holding their hats in their hands. Among them was David Jones, incognito as always.

The harbour and the new ship were unusually silent.

The wind rose again. The masts pitched sideways. The two men on the bowsprit lowered themselves down and sat on it, holding a rope.

As the funeral cortege moved away, the men on the new ship raised their caps in the direction of Cricieth before placing them back on their heads.

Two hours later, the stallions saw a small old church before them. They had turned off the main road in Pentre Felin and were now traversing a track which led to the church of Ynyscynhaearn.

Before the coming of William Madocks, who created Tremadog and Porthmadog by building two embankments and driving back the sea, this village of PentreFelin was near the sea's edge and this church was virtually on an island. It was still only accessible at medium and low tide. Farmers and village residents were buried here and services were held in Welsh and English.

Now, a service in Welsh marked the passing of their local poet. He who had known all the local families and written short poems in memory of those passed away. His work was on hundreds of gravestones. The people's heritage was in this church. It had seen centuries come and go.

Around the church, humble gravestones marked the names and homes of those who had drowned at sea; the grave empty of the remains of a body, occupied by stones which had been placed in the coffin *in lieu*. Very few of these graves were elaborate; they were mostly small slate slabs, undecorated.

The line of mourners went back from the church, through the gate and down to the stream. They sang three hymns in Welsh and they recited the Lord's Prayer. The music rippled against the landscape and carried over to the nearby beach.

The coffin was lowered. The minister read Ioan's famous englyn *Crist y Meddyg*:

> *Pob cur a dolur drwy'r daith – a wellheir*
> *Yn llaw'r meddyg perffaith;*
> *Gwaed y groes a gwyd y graith*
> *Na welir moni eilwaith*

(Every pain and sore through our journey / are improved in the hand of the perfect doctor; / The blood of the cross cures the wound / that will not be seen a second time.)

A month later, an observer at the church would have noticed, close to the front door, a new column of pink Italian marble, about six feet high, and on it the name of John Williams, 'Ioan Madog' with his dates of birth and death. There had been a collection, mostly at his favourite pub The Ship, and the cost was covered by contributions from 'the working poor'. He was honoured by his people.

As one door closes, another opens.

In the meantime, the sea was flowing in to Porthmadog harbour. The *C.E.Spooner* was straining at her ropes. A launching platform had been built off the harbour wall. On it was Mr C.E.Spooner. He was wearing a dark overcoat and a tall black hat. His silver beard and the hair of his head fell against his coat.

He stepped forward. All those gathered around the harbour looked up. He took the bottle which was hanging by a rope from the ship's deck. He swung the bottle in his right hand and brought it crashing against the bow. The bottle splintered and its content of red wine streamed down the ship's flank

"I name this ship the *C.E.Spooner*," he said in strong tones. The wind had abated and the ship was quietly upright.

The assembled sailors and onlookers cheered.

Tynna'r rhaffau (remove the ropes) came the shout and two sailors stepped forward on the quay. The ropes were unfastened and pulled aboard, their tails in the water. The engine in the *Wave of Life* tugboat changed into a deep roar as she took the strain.

The tall ship with her naked masts moved forward and was towed through the harbour entrance.

An hour later, her sails were employed in the westerly wind at the bar. With her cargo of slate, she was making her way to Hamburg, Germany. She was heading south, along Cardigan Bay, towards Plymouth and the English Channel

The sea; the purpose; the energy; the sails.

The day had seen the best of it and the worst of it. There had been a death, and then the magnificent counterpoint, there had been a birth.

Chapter 20

"THROW US an orange," shouted Iwan H. Jones.

Iwan had just put on his brown suit and was looking forward to visiting Falmouth for the first time.

They had passed the *C.E.Spooner* at anchor; she looked fit and well, and perhaps a little smug.

But now the Fowey barquentine *T.E.Hocken* was drawing alongside and the first thing they experienced in the *Excelsior* was the smell. It wasn't unpleasant but it was foreign. It was the smell of citrus fruit which had been carried in the confined space of a ship's hold for about two weeks. She had come from the Canaries. Lemons, oranges and small Canary bananas were her cargo, stored where there was plenty of cooling air in straw filled open-plank containers. It was a chancy business. Too much hot air and rot set in quickly. And then the gin-and-tonics through England would have a shortage.

From a dark-capped mariner came a flash of orange. Iwan caught the fruit with his left had.

"And another for my friend," he shouted again and another orange came over.

"Very good. Our thanks," he shouted and the friendly mariner on the large *T.E.Hocken* raised his arm. His vessel was in good shape, almost as if she had just come from Truro, a few miles away.

Ahead of them as they came to the entrance to Falmouth was the headland Pendennis Point, to their left. On its highest point was an old castle. It looked rather run-down and untidy. 'Not a patch on Cricieth or Harlech,' thought

Iwan, or the huge Caernarfon castle which his father had taken him to one day.

Thinking of the home bay with its two castles set him looking at the present setting, with another castle over to his right; St Mawes Castle, which was little more than a ruin. But it was like home. They took a good look at Black Rock, which emerges in the centre of the approach, and sailed in to the right of it. By chance, Iwan was from Morfa Bychan. Each day as he rose from his bed in the stone farmhouse, he looked down to the sands they called Black Rock. Each day, the sea was his friend, stretched out before him and he loved it, whatever the weather.

He took to sea, as did so many sturdy young men from small arid farms.

The brig moved surely, carrying only two square sails on the mizzen. Falmouth looked good. Its many inlets and bays had a surprising amount of grass and trees. It reminded him of the estuary below his house in Y Garth.

It wasn't long before the ship was tied to the shore and Iwan stepped down the gangplank.

"A place for good food and a bed for the night," he asked an old longshoreman who was enjoying a plug of tobacco.

"Aye, aye." His face was severely wrinkled but his blue eyes were lively.

"The Crow." He nodded his head. "Yonder."

Henry followed his directions and entered a inn conveniently set at the harbour entrance. He announced his name and occupation to the publican. It was arranged that dinner would be served in an hour's time and the youthful mariner was taken to his room.

Out of the bedroom window he could see the *Excelsior* nodding quietly at anchor and next against Fishstrand Quay was the *T.E.Hocken*, looking much bigger.

"A Westindiaman" was how the barquentine was called in the bar room. It was a convivial place; plenty of talk and good humour.

"Where ye sailed from," he was asked.

"Porthmadog," he replied.

"That place that makes ships," his companion asserted.

"Yes. Yes indeed. Plenty of them and they are good and strong."

"Look at that *Hocken*," the man replied. "She is a looker. That long, low, wedge-like bow. But that *C.E. Spooner*. Is she one of yours?"

"A Porthmadog schooner. Built on Cei Newydd by David Jones. There is talk that she has crossed the north Atlantice in thirteen days."

The air in the bar room seemed to change. "Thirteen days," was repeated by the assembled mariners and ex-mariners.

"The wind must have been regular and true," said another bearded man.

"And the ship," replied Iwan, and they all murmured agreement.

He slept well that night.

Chapter 21

CHARLES EASTON was standing on the lawn at Bron-y-Garth. The day was fine, with large clouds. The walls of Harlech castle stood out against the distant shore. It was a good day for sailing.

His eyes scanned the sea to his right and in a few moments a brown blur on the horizon was recognizable as a sailing vessel approaching. He turned and went through the large wooden door at the Porthmadog end of the building, picking up a telescope from the hall stand. Opening it and placing it to his eye, he focused on a ship with sails, a jack barquentine. She was making good progress for in a minute his eye picked up a brown shape on the ship's bow. It gleamed and sparkled in the sun. Across the bows he picked up a name in white – *C.E.Spooner.* The brown shape was an effigy of himself, in copper. It was attached to the ship on its second voyage, not having been finished for attaching at first launch.

A wave of pleasure swept through him. Only once before in his eventful life had something given him such palpable pleasure (when the *Little Wonder* exceeded all expectations and swept up to Blaenau in great style). He stood there with the glass to his eye for five minutes, enjoying the event. The square sails on the foremast were in bulbous shape; the fore-and-aft sails were down, except the one on the lower mizzen, which was effective in making sure the route to harbour was followed. He saw one, then two, square sails, being lowered. He saw the helmsman standing behind the large teak wheel. The vessel was in proud shape. She was painted black, with a yellow strake along the gunwale, copper bottomed with a white strake along the top of the copper.

He had heard a whisper, but he was not sure. That she had come across the north Atlantic very fast: "quick" was the word they used. Across Porthmadog harbour many voices, especially those of the builders of ships, echoed the story: the *C.E.Spooner* had done something very special. A quiet pride lay across the harbour.

The pilot boat had set out from its moorings on the peak of the bay of Borth y Gest and was now alongside the *Spooner*. The pilot took over the controls. He knew the intricacies of the sands and the tides at the joining of the rivers Dwyryd and Glaslyn. Through his spyglass, Charles Easton saw the vessel change angle and the boom at the rear change direction. She slowed as the wind dropped. But her route was safe and well-directed. She came closer to Bron-y-Garth. Two sailors stood on deck facing him. They raised and shook their caps. As the barquentine with its three tall masts passed below his house, with the copper figurehead of himself as a younger man on its bow, a picture was formed in his mind of this unique scene, which never left him. It was a beautiful day.

The following morning, at seven, there was a vigorous knock on the front door of Bron-y-Garth. One of the maids answered and ushered the two in to the front parlour. Catherine Jones sat in an upright chair. William Jones, Master of the *C.E.Spooner*, sat in a comfortable armchair and spread his brown hands over both arms.

Charles Easton entered. It was as if he had lost ten years. It was a sprightly Charles who shook both vigorously by hand.

"I have heard," he said. "We heard last night. You have set the record for crossing the north Atlantic."

"I believe we have," said William, his young face set in a mask of pride. He was still holding Charles's hand when he asserted, "It was a crossing of great luck; everything was for us – the winds, the temperature and the right crew."

"You had the right spread?" asked the older man.

"Certainly," replied William. "A simple one but it was maximum for speed. Fore topmast staysail, lower topsail, double reefed mainsail, no mizzen sails."

"Sit," said Charles. "We shall have a drink to celebrate."

Even the normally abstinent Catherine Jones was not opposed, on this occasion.

Charles gave the order and a bottle of Williams and Humbert sherry was brought from one of the deeper cupboards in the kitchen. It came from Jerez and Williams was a Welshman. He put his hand around the bottle. "Not too cold, as it would have been if stored in the cellar," he said.

The best cut-glass small glasses were produced and Charles poured each glass slowly.

"This is a fine achievement," he said. "I am pleased. Very pleased. But how was it done?"

William replied, "It would have been my brother's voyage, but he had to deal with the family farm in Minffordd ... and even though I have only a 'fore and aft' certificate, I was glad to take over. I knew straight away that this was special. I have never known a ship in such good spirits. She was desperate to go to sea, straining at the leash. And my mate and hands were fit and afraid of nothing. As you know, sailing a three-master requires special qualities in the men, and this time, they were determined. From the beginning, we were making fast progress. We sailed to Hamburg with slate in five days. We knew there was salt in Cadiz so we sailed there in ballast.

Cadiz is a handy place. It is an old city built on a spit so you can get to harbour on both sides, saving time. We took on water and supplies, and the cargo of salt, well-packed, and set off westwards across the Atlantic, for Harbour Grace, Newfoundland."

The confidence and knowledge of this young man came over strongly to Charles and the businesslike Catherine Jones. They could see why his men trusted him.

"When you have three masts and a combination of square and fore and aft, you can adjust according to the conditions and you can go very fast. And this time we were lucky. The crew were used to brigs and schooners but this time with two large sails on the main and mizzen and square sails on the fore, the crew merely had to step up. Beating against the north Atlantic is far better in a ship with this combination of sails."

William spoke with the knowledge of a man who had been through it.

"We came in to Harbour Grace with time to spare. The air smelled of fish. We needed to pick up and get out. We were told as we were making fast that the place we needed to be was Shoal Bay, Labrador, where a huge amount of cod was waiting to be shipped. So we wasted no time. The next morning we sailed for Labrador and when we arrived, they were right. There must have been at least ten vessels waiting to load."

The talk of such a distant place made the two listeners quiet. They had no experience of the Atlantic, and the east coast of Canada. It was another world.

"Carrying fish is better than most cargo. It is lighter and more valuable. In the Catholic countries they do not have enough from their own fisheries, so we bring it to them by ship. We have the fish in tall barrels, which are easy to load and stack. We had plenty of salt, so we shovelled it in to the barrels with the fish, and when they were all loaded, we covered it all over with salt, then tied it all down with tarpaulin."

The two listeners were fascinated.

"And it was a smooth crossing of the North Atlantic. The trade winds blew night and day. As we passed Gooseberry Island, the speed of travel was outstanding. And it stayed that way. Our crew was determined. Hardly anything went wrong. Our steward was happy in his cooking. Everybody had his six hours' sleep. Sails were set for the prevailing wind which did not change too often. The double mainsail was working very hard all the way. On the sixth day, we thought we were heading for a storm. The sky blackened and the wind rose."

The two listeners sat forward in their chairs.

"But it passed us by. It actually helped us on our way. Then in the early morning, the watch shouted 'Land. Land.' We knew, or hoped it was, Ireland. The shore of County Cork. We knew we were right when we saw the Fastnet. This is a spur of rock off the south-west corner of Ireland, with a lighthouse on it. We sailed close to it, and as we passed, I took a bearing and noted in my diary: 'From Shoal Bay, Labrador to Fastnet Rock, Ireland, thirteen days, four hours, twenty-one minutes'."

"A record," said Charles. "The previous best sail crossing was by a Falmouth schooner, in fifteen days."

"And we have our fish, intact," said the punctilious Catherine Jones.

Chapter 22

THE INDIAN OCEAN was home to *Pride of Wales*. She was Simon Jones's masterpiece and there was something extraordinary about her.

She represented a new type of design of ship. She was a departure from anything Porthmadog and Borth y Gest had attempted before. The tonnage exceeded previous efforts. She could carry a dead weight load of over 500 tons. With a length of 125 feet, a breadth of 26 feet and a depth of 14 feet, she was a real deep-water ship. She was big, sturdy and full of purpose.

Barque-rigged, and with the lighter stay-sails and stun' sails set, she was seen scudding along the tropical waters of the Indian Ocean with twenty-six sails spread across the sky.

Running along the centre line of a thirty-foot poop, the wheel, wheel box, and deck gratings, companion way, binnacle stand, decorative skylight and the booby hatch of the lazaret, were made of varnished teak, heavily ornamented by brass fittings. A six-stand bucket rack of the same material enclosed the fore-part of this dignified retreat. Four-inch whitewood planks, the seams of which were filled with red putty, formed the poop deck, which was surrounded at intervals by fancy shaped stanchions festooned by a white-painted chain. Two toy cannons were lashed on the quarters, one on each side. As the poop was approached from the main deck the centre panel of the 'break' carried a heavy carving of the Royal Coat of Arms, picked out in rich colours and tipped with gold. The poop steps were of varnished teak with brass treads and white cord lanyards as hand-rails. The main deck close to the break of the poop was bridged by boat skids with the davits on the starboard side. Between the after hatch and the main fife-rails on the centre-line, a full-sized capstan stood with its bars in a tidy rack close by. All the fittings on the main deck were on a central line so that an uninterrupted run could be got on either side as far as the spacious fo'castle head which mounted another capstan. So perfect was her curve that a two-foot ruler placed on its edge on any part of the deck, on a fore and aft manner, would show the proportionate degree of curve over the given distance.

As she approached, the graceful flare of her bows gave a buoyancy which anticipated and smashed the breaking sea however angry it might be.

She was on charter to the Indian Government. It was this that excited Shon Edwards when he drew a jungle scene, a representation of most of the reptiles that dwelt in the Burma marshes, some hiding in, others squirming through tropical reeds and grasses, but all expressing savage displeasure at being taken to sea.

She was carrying cargo of the dry, non-bulk sort: crates, trunks, boxes and mail from Ceylon. She was *en route* to her home port of Chittagong. As she approached the sacred river, The Ganges, the sunset behind her flared in her sails with the orange and gold of India.

Chapter 23

THE MAN in the grey suit on the gangplank of *Pride of Wales* represented the British Empire. Behind him holding his leather travel cases were two sailors.

Behind them was the barque in relaxed mode, gently swaying. Her green paint was a little worn and the gold strake around her middle was missing in places.

He represented the best of the Spooners of Porthmadog. Born in 1853, he was the fourth child and third son of Charles Easton Spooner of Bron-y-Garth, Borth y Gest.

He looked around the busy harbour. Colombo, the capital of Ceylon, had been a shipping and trading centre for many hundreds of years. This was natural because it lay on the main shipping route between Europe, the Middle East (before the Suez Canal) and the lucrative states of India and the Far East. Ships from a variety of countries lay at harbour. He was standing, he knew, on the route of the spice trade, which in England had created fortunes for traders in London and Bristol.

This ship and this young man were exemplary. He had graduated in engineering at Trinity College, Dublin, much to the pleasure of his father, and had accepted a position in the survey department of the Council of Ceylon. He was not one for joining the family business of railways in Porthmadog. Percy had a gift for drawing, so Percy would remain at home and he, Edwin, would strike out for foreign parts.

Edwin had the gift of presence. He had charisma. He was always well-dressed: he had a steady look in his eyes. He spoke economically, controlled but not without feeling.

Charles Edwin Spooner was a man going places.

The bustle of the harbour before him, he adjusted his tie. His suit was well-cut and his shoes were black, bespoke. He was wearing a silk-grey homburg which was set squarely over his eyes, not the tall black hat of the previous generation.

"Let us find Mr Harrison. Mr Logue-Harrison," he announced to the two sailors. Three-quarters of the way down the gangplank, he thought he saw the man. He was stationed a few yards from the foot, looking upwards. He wore a brown suit with a waistcoat embellished with a gold double chain. Such decoration was for the older sort, thought Charles Edwin: we younger, more fashionable, ones go for the plainer look.

As Charles Edwin stepped on to the soil of Ceylon, the brown-suited man stepped forward.

"Greetings. Greetings. I am Henry Logue-Harrison. Welcome to the Empire State of Ceylon. As her Majesty's Representative, I welcome you."

"Thank you," said Charles, with a constrained bow.

"Did you have a good trip?"

"We started at Amsterdam, in a clipper. *Pride of Wales* was at port in Lisbon, When I stepped aboard, I felt that I was in my home town. I had a good long bunk and some fine company in the Welsh captain and his mate, The sailors sang songs and shanties. We had the great heat off Africa, where we docked at Freetown, taking on food and water. There were a couple of rough days going round the Cape; Durban was a pleasure. Then, with plenty of water to drink, we crossed the Indian Ocean in great style. After a week or so she will cross the Bay of Bengal to Chittagong, and from there to Rangoon and then to Sourabaya. She's a fine vessel," replied Charles.

"Well done, old chap. Well done."

Charles Edwin was used to ships so the usual turbulence was not exceptional . Brought up on the edge of the Irish Sea in a house full-on to the wind, the disturbances associated with sea and wind were natural to him.

"Call me Harry. I am sure we shall get on very well."

This man, thought Charles, is not quite the Empire Administrator he had expected. But in his mind Charles knew that Harry was more able and more significant in getting things done than the usual Raj model. There was an intelligence, drive and directness about him. He was not a smooth pretender, merely striking attitudes, like many of the other Empire representatives, with their fancy headgear and glittering uniforms.

"Let us move on," said Henry. "Please," and he addressed the two sailors, "take Mr Spooner's luggage to the roadway, there." He pointed to where a carriage was drawn up, with three Sinhalese servants on display.

Settled in the carriage, Charles admired *Pride of Wales* waiting at anchor. She looked at at home in the Indian Ocean.

The vessel lay proudly in harbour. She was a representative. She carried the Royal coat-of-arms. As the bay geldings moved the carriage forward in a smooth and orderly motion, Charles Edwin, aged only twenty-three, was turning a corner in to a new life. If that life turned out to be as well-made and attractive as the ship built on a narrow strip of land in small Borth y Gest, he would be fulfilled and happy.

Chapter 24

ON THE highest point of Y Garth, Porthmadog, where the road flattens-out for two hundred yards or so, the house of David Morris, ship-owner, stood large and multiple. It was being enlarged to accommodate the children of David's daughter, Jenny Morris and her husband William Garth Hughes, Master Mariner. Jenny's figurehead on the *Pride of Wales* stood for increase and profit, which is what was happening. Since her marriage and honeymoon on the brig *Excelsior* in 1871, she had children. Her father David Morris enjoyed the fruits of his investments in local ship-building and trading. It was a risky business, investing in ships, but he had been lucky. The sloop *Success* was well-named. And after the schooner *Ocean Monarch* was built by Simon Jones in 1851, David Morris made ten years of income out of her, then sold her to his brother-in-law. The schooner *Royal Charter* followed, the only ship built at Abergafran, Minffordd, in 1858; she was sold and later capsized off Bardsey in 1880. Then came *Pride of Wales* and she was making large and regular amounts of money on the Indian Ocean. It was not surprising that David Morris retired from sea-going at an early age.

As *Pride of Wales* traded between Colombo in Ceylon and Chittagong in east India, crossing the Bay of Bengal, it was not surprising that the money she made for her owner was invested in a house named Ceylon Villa. This house, through the beneficence of the Morris family, later, after more expansion, became Porthmadog Hospital.

At the Borth y Gest end of this flat road stood the curving stone entrance, wooden gate and stone low-roofed bungalow lodge, of the entrance to Bron-y-Garth. Its curving drive was flanked by laurels and bushes, and the gardens on three sides of the spacious house was tended by a team of gardeners.

All was not well at Bron-y-Garth. Turning towards the house at the end of the drive, a man was to be seen sitting on a wooden seat by the balustrade. He was facing the estuary. From the back, he could be seen to be wearing a suit of fine check and a cream shirt. His hands lay across the rim of the seat and his cuff-links caught the sun.

The house was unusually quiet. It was as if the occupiers were away on holiday. But they were not. It was a curious state to be in. The news concerning Percy had come as a shock and a silence prevailed.

Percy raised his right hand and pulled it across his forehead. He stared across the estuary with a frozen look.

He had not expected this. Not at all. His dalliance with Eleanor had not been insistent or intense, just occasional, and he had not expected any consequence. But Eleanor was pregnant. And Percy was in trouble and in shock.

As he looked at the cob and the flowing of the Glaslyn and Dwyryd, words said by his father yesterday burrowed in to his mind.

"We cannot stomach it." Stomach seemed appropriate. "We cannot go on as normal. This is an established, respectable, household. We cannot have a maid with child and my son responsible. We have to make provisions. I shall set my mind to it. And you will take your responsibilities. You have made your bed. So you lie in it."

The power of this metaphor struck deep in to Percy.

His father was adamant, and his rule was law.

A week later, Charles Easton Spooner had a plan.

"India," he said. "The Eastern Bengal Railway. About eighty miles is being built out of Calcutta. There is confidence that the State of India will take over the running and ownership of the railway soon. They are looking for trained engineers. I have a contact in the India office. You are to see him on Tuesday of next week in London."

So, the ultimatum was laid down.

Percy followed his father's instructions. In London he explained his qualifications; educated at Harrow, trained in engineering at Karlsruhe Polytechnic, apprenticed at Boston Lodge: designed the Festiniog Railway locomotives *James Spooner* and *Myrddin Emrys*. Worked with Fairlie. His father had worked under Isambard Kingdom Brunel. The mere mention of that name caused the room to change its mood.

"But have you travelled abroad?" asked the Indian envoy. "No," replied Percy. "But I have a brother in Ceylon."

"You have excellent credentials and of course your father is a distinguished engineer. We want men of substance. Somebody who can give orders, command respect, and handle the native ways and the climate. This is a new project. There are many obstacles to be overcome. The Ganges is huge and unpredictable. The job has to be done. Otherwise the area, with its big population, will fall in to poverty and starvation."

The small man before him pulled no punches. Percy respected him for his directness. Practical solutions suited him well at this crucial stage of his life.

Percy asserted, "It will be a challenge. But my family have thrived on challenges. Creating a railway to run up a mountain is no easy task. My grandfather and father did that."

There was a pause. "The position is yours," the envoy announced. You will sail from London on the twenty-fifth. I shall make all the arrangements. There will be other India Office men and families sailing with you.

I hope your wife and yourself will enjoy the voyage."

The matter of 'wife' had been kept quiet. In reality, there was no wife. They were to be married later, quietly.

Back in Bron-y-Garth, the change in Percy's life was taking

time to sink in. No longer the chief man in Boston Lodge design section; no longer a protected son of Charles Easton Spooner; no longer the designer of excellent locomotives. No longer the luxury of Bron-y-Garth. The break was painful and absolute.

Eleanor was anxious. The trip to London worried her and the long sea-voyage worried her even more. She was not a natural traveller. She would have liked nothing better than to marry a local man and bring up her children in the shadow of Moel y Gest.

However, she was not blind to the possibilities before her. She would have a respected husband holding down a good job. She would have accommodation provided, with servants. Her child would have comfort and security in growing up. She believed they would be happy.

A four-horse carriage came to take them away. Everybody was well dressed. Their four trunks were loaded. The family and servants stood by the front door.

Percy and Eleanor shook hands with John, James and Mary.

Louisa said, "We love you both. Have a good journey and enjoy India. Let us know how you get on. We shall expect a letter from you soon."

Charles Easton was not so open. He felt the responsibility of having created this break in the family line.

"All the best to you both," he said as they entered the carriage.

Hands and arms were raised in greeting as the gravel on the drive crunched beneath the carriage wheels. The laurels swayed as the four horses passed down the drive in unified movement.

The air behind them seemed to separate, forming a vacuum. The change was huge and absolute.

Chapter 25

THE FIRST OF July 1884 was an important day for Percy and all his colleagues on the Eastern Bengal Railway.

"The addition of a name. Just a little word," he said.

"State. What a strong word. It means country, government. And it means ownership," said his friend Paul. "We are now employed by the State. We should feel more secure. Perhaps Queen Victoria will come to see us."

"She can sit in one of our new First Class carriages," replied Percy.

Paul had been here for some fifteen years. There was no doubt that he was a good railwayman and a good leader of men. It was he who had designed the badge of the railway. A belt with a buckle at the bottom, a crown sitting on top to mark the Raj, a jungle scene with an elephant, and in the centre a locomotive steaming to the right.

"I shall have to change the device. I shall have to take out 'Eastern Bengal Railway' and put in 'Eastern Bengal State Railway 1884'," said Paul.

"You are the artist, the designer. I am sure you will create something suitable," said Percy, smiling.

Percy turned to the assembled railway management and their wives. He spoke with a measured earnestness: "Then there are the other sections. There is the Calcutta and South Eastern Railway. I am sure that in a year or so there will be a joining and then the badge will stand for a bigger railway. We have much scope here. This East Bengal is complicated territory. We are needed here. We have to drive forward. We are faced with the Ganges in all her size and moods and we have to overcome obstacles. There is huge population and much poverty. We have to get the goods to market. Jute to the coast and exported by sea. And then we must think of the Assam mountain area. Tea is a major commodity and needs to be taken by ship to the ports of the world, Europe and especially England. Trade is expanding at a quick rate ..." His views had an appreciative audience. His colleagues and their wives nodded their heads with approval. His wife Eleanor looked at him with admiration. She looked attractive in her pale cream dress and blue hat. Percy put his arm around her waist and with the other he placed it on the head of their daughter Kitty, whose brown eyes and black hair made her appearance more akin to that of their Indian colleagues. Kitty looked up at her father, whom she adored.

Chapter 26

Percy SPOONER and the East Bengal State Railway was something of a talking point in Porthmadog. Very little was known in certainty but when a vessel sailed to berth at the port, a small drizzle of information came with the ship, originating in the Bay of Bengal.

Back in Porthmadog, on the 11th of October 1886 Johnnie Williams was on the edge of the most important journey of his life. It was he who had stood next to his father as a boy, watching their miniature locomotive Topsy run around the garden of Bron-y-Garth.

"Dad," he said to his father. "The railway here is well settled now. You are in charge and it is going according to Mr Spooner's wishes."

William Williams was proud of his son. There was a sturdiness about him and he was able to make decisions.

William Williams replied, "Yes. We have achieved. We are known in the world. We have made strides with locomotives and the Fairlie has placed us on the map. You are making the right decision. We shall miss you."

Mrs Elizabeth Williams was wearing her best outfit, including a blouse of silk.

They were both people of importance. William was recognised for his excellence in engineering. He had been appointed Superintendent of Railways and given rent-free accommodation on the railway at Boston Lodge. His father, another William Williams, had passed away and he missed his knowledge of engineering and advice. His grandfather was the legendary Richard Williams, the blacksmith of Tremadog who invented the moving platform that carried rock during the building of Madocks's second causeway, the cob.

"A long journey," said Johnnie. He picked up his leather case and his canvas hold-all. "I hope I am not sick at sea."

"You will be well," said his father. "You are joining one of the new railways of the world. Percy Spooner is an able man. We had him here and he was an excellent draughtsman. He knew what he was doing. He will be your friend and I am sure a fair employer. There is much work to do there. Bengal is very populated and they need good people to be engineers and administrators."

"Will I be an able administrator?" replied Johnnie. The engineering came to him through his blood.

"I am sure you will be," replied his father. "Work hard. Be systematic. And be fair with people."

They were standing at the gate of their stone cottage. William stepped forward and pressed a £5.00 note in to Johnnie's hand.

Johnnie turned towards the main street. He observed gangs of workers putting up new telegraph poles along High Street. Perhaps I shall be able to use those and send a message, he thought. He reached the Royal Sportsman Hotel and turned in to the yard at the side. Stepping in to the Chester coach, he knew that behind him was a community the likes of which he would never experience again. It was a powerhouse. It carried slate, it created ships, it traded in all the items required for the maritime business, it had its own bank and its own insurance company. And it was only born around 1800, when Madocks came here. When there was fire in a Welshman's belly, thought Johnnie, there wasn't much he and his friends couldn't accomplish. Perhaps he could start a fire in India.

He travelled to London where at the Port he stepped on the deck of a clipper bound for Lisbon. The world was opening up before him. Behind him was a community whose values were based on truth, hard work and mutual trust.
He hoped he would find at least some of this in the Bengal that he was heading for.

Chapter 27

THE NOVEMBER sky over Porthmadog was still and quiet. A few stragglers in the distance were walking across the cob. The Moelwyn mountains were as if they had been painted on a theatre stage. The sharp-edged Cnicht was narrower and more sweeping than usual. The Glaslyn was sluggish, running against its icy banks under snow-covered overhanging bushes.

The Festiniog Railway was silent. Its carriages were lined-up in tidy order; its locomotives sitting inside, where oil and grease was turning colder and less tractable. Men who usually had their sleeves rolled up, wearing old waistcoats, who worked in the engineering shed with iron and steel, were now wearing their Sunday suits and their fob chains.

The man who had guided them for over thirty years had died last night.

All the engineering activity was as the blood in his veins. Now the engine had stopped; his life had stopped.

The man's face was as a ghost before them. The tall bare forehead, the strong eyes, the sideways-flowing beard, the commanding voice. This was gone. He had taken his last breath in Bron-y-Garth, in the bedroom with brown striped wallpaper.

"Father," John Eryri said. "We have all depended on you."

"Yes," came the reply.

"The railway and the town," said John. "All the business of slate."

"Slate," echoed Charles Easton.

"We are here in Bron-y-Garth where you brought us."

"Yes."

"Percy and Edwin are abroad. They are carrying on the business."

"The business," came the reply. "Porthmadog. The mountain. Engines."

The voice was weaker.

"We owe much to you, Father," said John.

His final words were, "Much. Much. We have done."

At this a stillness came over the face. In the distance, seagulls cried.

They stood around the bed.

"Father has gone," said John Eryri.

Chapter 28

IN CEYLON, Henry Logue-Harrison was a man of importance. He was brisk. He had a sense of what needed doing. He was strongly loyal to Queen and Empire.

He lived in a large pink-painted house at the leafy back of Colombo. His office was in a front room and from here he could see the city in all its variety, people and landscape. In the distance he could see the sails of tall ships.

"Edwin, old chap," he addressed Charles Edwin Spooner. "We have to find a wife for you. A young man in these parts needs a good companion. Damn it, you have been here a good ten years now. You are well respected. You don't want to be on your own do you?" He raised a quizzical eye.

"No," said Edwin. "But the opportunity has not arisen."

"But we shall have to make opportunities," asserted Henry. He was on the point of ringing the bell, summoning a maid, and asking his wife to come here. He thought perhaps they could arrange a dinner and invite eligible ladies. But he thought again. It was a crude move.

"Perhaps I am not the type," said Edwin, after staring at the fireplace. "I am not much of a social animal."

"But you are very charming," Henry asserted. "People like you. You are good with people. Surely you need home comforts."

"This is the social self," replied Edwin. "At home I am very satisfied. I have good friends." He smiled to himself.

"You have gone from the Survey department to the Department of Public Works. You have advanced. And Ceylon has advanced. You are a railways man but your design and planning skills are now in evidence all over the island. Roads are improving and now planning and housing are much more controlled and orderly. History will tell what you have given these people. A trained mind; that's what they needed." Henry was very explicit and very praising. He was not one to be understated about achievements, especially not ones done by the British.

"I shall make my way home," said Edwin.

"Take the best carriage," said Henry. "You need to cut a dash among these people."

"No," replied Edwin. "I shall walk."

Henry looked at him with a mixture of puzzlement and respect.

"Your house is still small. Have you found a better one yet?" said Henry who had actually never been to Edwin's residence in a less salubrious part of the city.

"I am looking," said Charles diffidently.

The large oak door with its little copper bell closed behind him as he walked the drive, leaving the pink house. His well-cut suit and hat stood out.

He passed the old Wolvendaal Church which had been designed and built by the Dutch. It reminded him of pictures he had seen in books of buildings in Florence.

He walked around Pettah Market, with its activities in trading. The brisk movements of buyers and sellers was a mosaic of sight and sound. He observed the detail of the Jami Ul Alfar Mosque, with its orange brick, cupolas and pale stone bandings. He saw here how it fitted in with the market traders, their colour and movement, and how different this was to the design of the old Dutch church.

He was heading towards the port area. Soon he noticed the pattern of masts and yardarms over the rooftops. He turned in to Albert Road; one which he had drawn out on paper in an attempt to impose order on the muddled pattern of old streets. He regretted that some of the small old wooden native houses had had to be demolished to make room for the new road. Access to the port was mostly down

Victoria Avenue nearby, a wide and gracious road which carried ship-bound goods.

He opened his metal gate. On each side of the narrow drive flowers were blooming. He took one in his hand and dropped the orange petals to the ground.

His young man Amir approached.

"Good day, Sir," he said with the air of one confident yet cautious of tone.

"Been on business. With Sir Henry. He is pleased."

Amir smiled. He had beautiful eyes, long black hair and even teeth.

"How is the work?" asked Edwin.

"Proceeding," replied Amir, who had a liking for strong English words. "We have five workmen. They have been hammering and plastering. I think they know what they are doing."

"Let's take a look," said Edwin.

They walked the path around the side of the house. At the rear, well away from the eyes of passers-by, Edwin was building what appeared to be a facsimile of a small Indian temple. Its windows had pointed tops and five pillars stood across its porch. They stepped inside.

"The tower is not quite finished," said Amir.

"I will ascend," said Edwin, smiling.

He held the handrail of the wooden balustrade with its fretwork panels. It curved up in a graceful swoop. He was at the height of the house, its multiple roofline before him. He stepped on two wooden planks, where the floor of the tower room was to be.

"I shall spend time up here," he said to Amir, who had stayed on the ground floor. "What a look-out! What a panorama!"

"Panorama," Amir repeated.

It was a six sided lookout room. When finished, it would have the traditional Indian tulip-shaped roof, topped with a weather-vane made by a local craftsman.

Edwin looked across at the harbour. Then he raised his eyes to the horizon. He stayed looking at it for a minute. He wished he had a telescope. For something this side of the horizon caught his eye and he stood very still.

She was a sailing ship, approaching.

Something about her was familiar. A barque, three masted. Her prow upraised with a strong bowsprit. She was carrying her cargo with a confident air.

As her studding sails swerved with the wind, Edwin had a picture in his mind. He recalled Borth y Gest, standing in the corner of the wood at Bron-y-Garth with his brother. Seeing at the other side of the bay the newly-built *Pride of Wales* at launch. He recalled her smooth slide in to the waters of the estuary. He recalled a young woman standing on a raised platform, her light hair shining in the sun. The shining new vessel slid in to the water, stern first, the figurehead painted on her prow, with its flowing yellow hair and its hand, raised, holding a rose, pointing to the landscape of Borth y Gest, its place of origin. Now, the same vessel with the same figurehead was heading in to the harbour of Colombo, Ceylon, on the other side of the earth, and he, a Welshman from Borth y Gest, was greeting it with joy, silently, the allure of the figurehead closing in upon him.

As the sun began to set on Colombo harbour and the figurehead on the approaching ship moved in to focus, Charles turned and shouted to Amir, "She's *Pride of Wales*. *Pride of Wales*."

"Sir, what is that?" replied Amir.

"A ship. A sailing ship. She was made in my home town. She is a Porthmadog ship."

"Porthmadog," replied Amir. "Porthmadog. Is that a place in England?"

"No," replied Edwin. "In Wales. Wales."

"Is that far from England?" questioned Amir.

"Quite far," said Charles as he descended the curving stairway. He smiled, "Quite far."

Chapter 29

THE FOLLOWING morning, early, Charles Edwin Spooner was to be seen walking towards the Colombo quayside wearing black trousers, brown shoes and a tweed jacket. His height brought him above the local men and his tall forehead caught the early morning sun. As he approached the port, the bustle in the streets increased and the carts were larger and horse-drawn.

From a distance he recognised her. There was something in her stance; she was long, at over 125 feet, and her width, at over 26 feet, gave her deck extra room for various fittings. Her three masts were tall, with thick spars for her square sails, now down. Two gold lines were painted around her, one on her bulwarks. Her figurehead was as striking as ever, its arm reaching upwards holding a red rose. When traversing the ocean, the wooden painted figurehead would be removed and stored in a mahogany box for safely, but when approaching harbour, two seamen would be detailed to put the piece back in to place, carrying it forward in its box, and fixing with brass screws.

Edwin stepped around the boxes and crates on the quayside, looking upwards. He saw two men on board, one wearing a flat cap and a white shirt. That must be John Griffith, captain, he mused. From Barmouth, with a good reputation. Who else is on board?

The figure on the deck stepped forward as he approached. An arm was raised. John Griffith had half expected the visitor for he had been told that one of the Spooner brothers was in Ceylon. The captain leaned over the bulwarks, between the strong tracery of ropes.

"Mr Spooner, I presume," he joked, after the story of Stanley and Livingstone.

"Of the Spooners of Borth y Gest," came the reply.

"I am pleased to see you. Come on board."

So he was soon sitting in the captain's cabin, with teak panelling and a mahogany table. Carefully-made cupboards surrounded them, their brass fittings well polished.

"A good voyage?" enquired Edwin.

"Yes. Fine. We have the Bay of Bengal in our hand. She sails it as if born here. She gets very hot and her body makes strange noises, but her timbers are sound and so far, no problems." He remembered to touch the wood of the table.

"You were re-fitted at Port. Newly caulked. Checked for poor nails. A1 at Lloyds." Charles Edwin was showing his knowledge.

"And four new sails. They don't last for ever," replied Captain Griffith. "One thing large sails don't like is salt on them and a lot of very hot sun."

Edwin was drinking tea out of a china cup, a rare event on a wooden ship. It had been prepared by the cook, Pritchard, who had his own galley by the mizzen mast. His iron stove was coal and wood fired and he had his own store.

There was a certain stiffness between them. John Griffith knew that he was talking to one of the representatives of Queen Victoria and a main man in the economic and social development of Ceylon. And in addition, he was the son of Charles Easton Spooner, the man who was central to the development of Porthmadog, which was now thriving with world trade in slate, through its vigorous shipping.

"Father passed away," said John Griffith, carefully.

"I could not be there, of course, but I wished I had. It's a long way, with months at sea," replied Edwin.

"Two months. Perhaps six weeks in a good ship, like this one," was the confident reply.

"Have you seen Colombo?" asked Edwin.

"Very little," was the reply. "Sometimes the mate and I

stay in a little guest house, just off the quay. We have not ventured further."

"You must come and visit us," was the confident invitation. "Spend a few hours at my home. Come today. I shall expect you for tea at four." It was an unusual attitude by Edwin who had never before invited anyone to his home.

"And bring everyone, all the crew. I shall send my man to guide you."

Some of the foreign crew had been paid off but the Caernarfonshire men were aboard. That the crew had been invited surprised and pleased John Griffith.

"They would be delighted. But I'll have to leave one behind, to guard the ship."

"Fine. How many is that?"

"The mate and me and five sailors," replied the captain.

"I shall expect all seven of you to my house. It will be a pleasure," said Charles with an unusual fulsomeness.

Soon the sailors were stepping down the gangplank, but not before all the slings and belays had been checked and the capstan was working properly. A young man from Cricieth had been left behind, and he was not pleased.

Hugh Pugh, the mate, was taking charge. He walked a few steps in front of the ordinary sailors, who were quiet and a little overawed by the privilege.

John Griffith and the young guide walked beside one another in front. As they walked the locals stepped aside and some of the older men raised their hands in respectful greeting.

They turned in to Albert Street with its private houses, lawns and overhanging trees.

They reached the point where the road turned. The guide stepped forward, turned sideways, raising his left arm.

"In here," he said and they proceeded along a narrow drive through an area of what appeared to be wild, uncultivated, land.

"And here it is, my home and Mister Spooner's."

They stood and took in the picture of a distinctly foreign house, with clap-boarding, shutters, multiple small windows and five or six roofs on different levels. There was something of the fairy-story about the house. It was not at all what they expected, such as the houses they had passed, with their large windows and airy spaces.

Assif answered the door bell. He had looked after Mr Charles Edwin for some ten years and he knew every nook and cranny of the property, including the wall at the rear which local small boys were inclined to climb over in pursuit of oranges and plums. Assif had a pile of sticks at the back of the garden for throwing at them.

"These are my friends," said Edwin, appearing in the hallway. "I have brought them here from their ship, *Pride of Wales*. Come in. Come in. We shall have tea and cakes."

Hugh Pugh was looking especially self-important. He stepped over the door mat sideways, as if boarding a ship.

They turned in to the drawing room, off the hall, which was floored in an Indian carpet of intricate design. Chairs had their backs to the walls but the centre of the room was dominated by a large low wooden table with curving legs and claw feet. Around the table were four sofas without backs, with pale blue cushions.

"We shall wash," said Edwin. In an adjoining room Assif prepared clean water in large bowls. Edwin washed his face, arms and torso, after removing his top clothes. After drying himself, he dipped his arms in a bowl of rosewater, splashing it on to his top half.

He dried himself, pulled on a fine linen garment, moved to the sofa and propped himself up, cross-legged.

The captain performed the same task but less rigorously, putting back his white shirt, but omitting his waistcoat. Hugh followed.

The five sailors, in a row, also washed, but only their faces and hands.

Assif entered, carrying a tray. On it was a large copper

unit with a curved handle. China cups and saucers were placed on the table along with a bowl of lose tea from Assam. Although local Ceylonese tea was acceptable, Edwin had developed a liking for the Indian variety.

Assif's nephew, a sixteen year old lad called Akram appeared with a tray of cakes. They were pink and white in the English way, with liberal coverings of icing. These cakes were kept under muslim cloths in a mesh-fronted cupboard in a dark corner of the kitchen, where they were treated with respect. Edwin liked his cakes and tea. To share them with others had never been known before.

"Gentleman," Edwin addressed the sailors. "Are you well?" They replied in low tones that they were. "Please help yourselves."

A silver spoon removed the tea from the bone china bowl. The tea was dropped in to the cups and very hot water was poured in from the copper urn. The sailors performed the task and sat silently, looking at the room. Each stooped forward, taking a cake, which he ate slowly, with relish.

Edwin looked relaxed. He looked like a different person. His long legs were ideally suited for the cross-legged position. He was lithe and athletic.

"Sailing is very challenging; it can be very enjoyable; and when the winds get up it can be hell." He addressed the sailors. "You are born to this," he said. "The long, long voyages without seeing land. The constant up and down of the sea. I saw an albatross once in the southern ocean. It is a moving sight. The singular loneliness of it, a thousand miles out to sea."

"We see them" said one of the sailors. "We like them. They are friendly and they are good luck."

Another sailor added, "The worst is the frost. It stops everything. Sometimes you have to hack it away to hoist the sails. And they are so heavy."

The conversation was loosening but John Griffiths did not want to outstay their welcome.

"We must get back to work," he announced.

Assif and Akram came in to clear away the tea things.

The sailors, Hugh and captain John rose to their feet with some difficulty. Charles Edwin rose to his feet in one swoop.

"Thank you. Thank you" said the sailors sincerely. Hugh Pugh boldly put out his hand. Edwin took it without hesitation.

"And many congratulations to you," said Edwin, turning to Captain Griffith. "You sail a fine ship and you have a loyal crew. Well done. I shall not accompany you back to the quay. You know the way."

He stood at the door as they left. Their last picture of him as they left was as a tall man, elegant, with fine manners. A man transplanted from a small town in north west Wales to a foreign country but representing something universal, beyond nationality. There is a certain dignity and style which belongs to the world.

The group of seven started their walk back to their ship. They were happy. One of them struck up a note. The others started humming. Soon all seven of them were singing to the rhythm of their walk. The song was *Dafydd y Garreg Wen*. It told of a young man who had lost his love and was picking up his harp again. The *garreg wen* was the large stone located in a field overlooking Borth y Gest harbour; and it was the name of a farm which was located between Borth y Gest and Morfa Bychan. When *Pride of Wales* was originally launched, its stern to the sea and its prow to land, it was pointing at the stone which jutted out of a sloping field some two hundred yards away. It was a beautiful tune, and it sounded especially resonant as it slid through the narrow streets of Colombo harbour.

Chapter 30

In 1891 David Williams and David Jones, shipbuilders, started their great rivalry. You could say there was bad blood there.

That blood had been spilt on the spit of land stretching out from the Rheilffordd Festiniog many years earlier. A seagull had started it. David Williams's failed aim with a stone caused it and ever after, David Jones, fiery, driven, intense, had nursed the scar on his arm as an emblem of control and ambition.

Both in their early 30's, both men had reached a point in their lives when knowledge, of the sea and its movements, of the intricacies of building wooden sea-going ships using local labour and supplies, had come together in to expression and outcome. Both men demanded nothing short of excellence.

On David Williams's yard, sideways on to the harbour, the *Dorothy* was being built: a three-masted schooner with top square sails. She was 142 tons; 91 feet long, nearly 23 feet wide, with a draft of close to 12 feet.

Blodwen was a three-masted schooner. David Jones and his men were tough and well-organised; they worked almost as if hypnotised, always together and always working quickly, producing a result before it could reasonably be expected. This *ad hoc* manner was helped by their location, closer to the entrance to the harbour. They could launch their ship directly into deeper water, whereas David Williams's ships had to be launched sideways.

The two Davids were similar in age and intention – to build the best Porthmadog ships. This similarity was evident in the names of their first two vessels, in the names: it extended through the design of both the *Dorothy* and the *Blodwen* which was the result of decades of Porthmadog/ Borth y Gest shipbuilding. Both ships were shorter than 100 feet; both had a width of just over 22 feet and both were practically identical in depth at 11 feet 6/7 inches. After some fifty years of shipbuilding this was the final, matured, almost identical, specification. The behaviour of this size of ship was the ultimate in cargo-carrying sea-voyaging efficiency. They could carry slate over oceans with ease and grace.

These were Western Ocean Yachts and there were to be 33 of them, all built by these two men and all built, two a year, until the last in 1913. It was a creative achievement, given the time and circumstances, never surpassed in the history of hand ship-building.

David Williams had presence. Medium height, with a muscular frame, a wide moustache and invariably a well-cut waistcoat, he drove his business forward with a firm orderliness. He believed in loyalty and trust, which is why he often worked on his ships with only four men and three boys, especially when fitting the inside, after the huge timbers for the frame had been bent, secured and the ship safely upright.

His four main men tended to copy his style. They changed their shirts every day and their waistcoats came from the same tailor in Porthmadog. David Williams sometimes in the summer wore a topi helmet in a light colour. This was copied by his men in that they sported light-coloured hats but in trilby style.

David Williams was considered a wealthy man. He had a successful career at sea and he lived with his wife and family in Porthmadog in a house not in a terrace but set in its own grounds. But wealth was relative. The average family lived on an income of hardly more than a pound a week. The average sailor was badly paid. David Williams had his expenses in shipbuilding – hiring his men, whom he paid well; buying the timber which was sometimes local and sometimes imported; fitting-out the ship with all the items necessary, including ropes and sails. Sails cost in the region of two hundred pounds per ship. He would charge in the region of two thousand pounds for building a new ship. He expected to make a profit of around £500 on each ship he built. So he lived well.

David, with his high cheekbones and dark complexion, adored his wife and family. He now had two daughters, Ellen and Constance. Both were outstandingly beautiful. They took after their mother who was a daughter of a farmer of Penrhyndeudraeth. David never hesitated in buying the best for them. In Porthmadog's High Street, the mother, Mary, and her two daughters were often seen in the shops, especially the milliner's, handling the newest fabric and trying on hats. lingering over the shelves of blouses They would buy a length of fabric, after much thinking and discussion, and take it to James the Tailor to have it made in to a new skirt or dress. They were proud people. There was no hesitation in asserting, as all the inhabitants of Porthmadog knew, barring discussion of David Jones, that David Williams was the best boat-builder that had ever been. His quality of work was the highest. He did not skimp. He was very particular in selecting the right wood, the right fittings. He built ships with the comfort and safety of their sailors in mind. When in distant ports, in San Francisco or Rio de Janeiro or Colombo, in the ships he built, their sailors would think of his and his men's sure hands.

Both daughters were brown-eyed and black haired. Both had strong-textured long hair. They brushed and combed it often, had it well cut, and usually tied it with ribbons on both sides. They were now growing in to young ladies and even though the local school afforded a minimum education, they seemed to have learned more than the usual share of knowledge, courtesy and style.

"*Bore da*," said Ellen, as she greeted Mrs Ellis, a neighbour, in the street. Her 'good mornings' were fulsome and sincere. She asked about Mr Ellis and his chest condition. "Please give him my best wishes," she asserted. For her age, she was remarkably assured.

"Now, what would our father like for supper?" asked Mary, holding her large shopping basket.

"Beef," said Constance.

"But beef is for Sundays," said Ellen.

"Chicken, then. I like chicken. Well done, with plenty of roast potatoes," replied Constance, who had no doubt about what she liked.

They entered Mr Rowlands's shop on the High Street. He had chickens and pheasant hanging in his window. Mary examined the chickens. She chose one with plenty of breast meat.

"That one," she said, pointing.

"And how are you today?" said Huw Rowlands, butcher. "And your lovely daughters?" He was never one to be short on flattery.

"My daughters are well-fed and growing strongly," she replied. "They are eating heartily."

Both girls smiled. They had faces that echoed one another.

Mary paid for the chicken and placed it in her basket.

Huw Rowlands continued, "I hear that Mr Williams is well ahead with the *Dorothy*. You can see it coming along every day. They tell me she is a new type of ship, shorter, fatter, capable of carrying large loads a long distance. We are very lucky to have men of Mr Williams's abilities in our new town. It makes life here. It brings in money over the counter."

At this the two sisters looked at one another. They were pleased to hear their father praised in such a positive way.

"He is a good man," replied Mrs Williams as she left the shop. "As are many others."

Chapter 31

SHOPPING FOR chicken in Porthmadog's High Street and facing the rains in East Bengal were highly contrasting activities. But George Percival Spooner was in his element. He was a naturally adventurous, bold man. He relished challenges. He had something of his father in him. He was prepared to take on a difficult, mountainous landscape, foul weather, engineering challenges and even a surly workforce, if he had the slightest chance of success.

He sat in the garden of his bungalow. He remembered the times in Bron-y-Garth. How his father had stood as the miniature train puffed around the garden. How Eleanor had emerged with the wine and how something had started in him towards her. How he sat in misery after learning of her pregnancy, his mind and spirit flattened with anxiety. How he left the house, bound for the Punjab, with the house behind him in a subdued state.

But his love for Eleanor had won through. It was the anchor of his life. She had settled with him in this far country with determination and adaptability. She had an open, honest manner, without superiority, and she was liked by everyone.

With him around the wicker table was Eleanor, his daughter Kitty, his colleague from many years ago, Paul Cameron and his new friend and local Porthmadog boy, John Williams.

They were a convivial group and the three men were a formidable team.

Two servants came forward with tea. They placed two silver urns containing very hot water on the table and two dishes of fresh Darjeeling tea. Eleanor liked sugar and milk in her tea, as did Kitty, but the three other men took it plain, without addition. The three were in discussion about railways.

"We have had the Eastern Bengal Railway and its line from Calcutta to Dacca, with a branch to Jessore. The Ganges was linked in with an extension to Kooshtee. Then we had the Eastern Bengal State Railway, and more capital came our way. Tea and jute is the main cargo for export, mostly through Chittagong. The problem is that the railways are not widespread enough, especially north, to cope with this traffic and expand it." Paul had long experience and a grasp of the economic realities.

"This is a huge and varied landscape," answered Percy. Water is our enemy and our friend. It may be that the three rivers, the Ganges, the Brahmaputra and the Meghna can be developed for freight, using schooners, which are shallow-drafted. This would put less need for building new railways on flood land."

"But this is not Porthmadog and the Ganges is not the Glasyn," chipped in Eleanor, smiling. She had no hesitation in joining-in the men's conversation.

"Certainly not," replied Percy. "And the population here is what they call – teeming."

"Plenty of workers, that's the need with railways. Digging, shifting, laying tracks, all sorts of manual work. We have that advantage here. When you say 'all hands on deck' they come in their hundreds," asserted Paul. "And they are good workers."

"That's because if they don't work, they starve," said Percy, grimly.

More tea was served.

"We have the Northern Bangal State Railway running up to Shiliguri, at the foot of the Himalayas. What we need is for goods and passengers to come down all the way to Calcutta without delays and change of trains. It is a dream," said Percy, adopting his firm speaking tone.

"The Darjeeling narrow gauge train is working well," he continued. "You should have been there, John. She is the same gauge as the Festiniog Railway which your father runs. And her track was surveyed by my father. He always called himself a railway engineer and the two-foot gauge was his ideal. The Darjeeling line is similar to the Festiniog. Plenty of gradients, woodland and rock, and sharp corners. Now she carries a great number of people. But the problem is that she cannot carry much freight; there isn't room. We need a bigger train on a wider gauge. And we can create that once we are down from the Darjeeling hills."

"The Darjeeling Railway will never carry enough freight. She is narrow-gauge. Her capacity is too small," said John, who had a close understanding of such railways. "But a powerful engine like the Little Wonder will make a big difference. We would need to have a number of them and run often."

Paul added, "The new rail connection between Santahar to Fulchari, ninety-four kilometers, is essential. Then we shall have jute and tea flowing down to Chittagong in quantities".

"And tea is huge," said Eleanor. "Every family in Great Britain has tea. It is our national beverage."

"I like tea," said Kitty. What she really meant was – she liked teatime.

Chapter 32

DAVID JONES was smaller than David Willliams and not as dapper. His manner was apparently random and uncontrolled; he was one of those men whose brain was well in advance of his actions.

He had been approached by Hugh Parry to build a new ship. Porthmadog was split in two – those who supported David Williams and those who supported David Jones. It was rather like the split between Nonconformists with their chapels and the Anglican church in Wales. Rivalries abounded at every turn. Some men would work for the one builder; other men would work for the other. And if one lost his job, rather than work for the other builder he would leave Porthmadog for Caernarfon or Liverpool.

David Jones was not easy to get on with. He was a bachelor. Nobody was quite sure where he lived, except that he appeared to be in lodgings somewhere down Madog Street. He emerged for his work in the very early morning; it could be five-thirty. He paced around his building yard, checking, moving, sawing, consulting the plans that he held under his arm and when his workers arrived for work, it would seem to him to be about the middle of the day.

He wore his bowler hat all day. His clothes were changed once a week. He had tall brown boots which he had worn for over a year.

Hugh Parry, shipbroker, of Porthmadog was a supporter of David Jones. He recognised his vigour, commitment and his passion, bordering on insanity, for building great ships.

"After my brother's first girl, we'll call her *Blodwen* said Hugh Parry. "She will be a Newfoundland Trader."

Building advanced at a quick pace. David Jones liked to hire a large number of men, usually not less than ten at a time, so that work moved forward quickly. When he was planking, the huge timbers cut from trees, steamed and bent in to position, he would have as many as twenty men, all pushing and straining at the timbers, arranging them in succession so that the flanks of the ship were even and symmetrical.

So the *Dorothy* and the *Blodwen* were being built within a stone's throw of one another, both ships unlike the previous sort. Both shorter, neater, less elegant in length but workmanlike in behaviour. David Williams's men worked systematically; David Jones's men worked vigorously. A combination of the two would make an ideal ship-building yard, but in reality they were separate, discrete and in competition. Men would stand, hands held flat above their eyes to see how the other was getting on. When a new delivery came, rope or webbing or even a pile of teak planks, speculation quickly ignited as to the use of such material. As for finish, it was generally allowed that David Williams had the best carpenters and the best contact with the local iron and foundry workers. The work of the deceased blacksmith and poet John Williams, known for his fine finish in metal, continued through his brother, with his tall frame and rectangular face – the man they called 'Beuno' – who had a workshop on the quayside.

Pride of Wales was the talisman. They were all proud of her. She was created beautifully and she behaved beautifully. And she was useful; she sailed the seas with no fuss; and she made a profit. She was the ideal Porthmadog ship until the creations of the two Davids came along. There was a type of breeding here: The *Pride of Wales* was the father ship; the *Blodwen* and the *Dorothy* were as her wives, who would produce strong, able children.

And so it was also with Jenny Morris. She had produced strong, able, children. Their house on the Garth – 'Ceylon

Villa' – had enlarged and enlarged as more children came to the family.

One of these was the young boy Henry Hughes. He was curious and fascinated by ships and the sea. When he placed his feet down on the ground when only seven months old, he walked with the gait of a seaman.

After many years in the East Indies, *Pride of Wales* sailed for England. In 1889 she left Colombo for Le Havre loaded with coffee. She was due for a Lloyd's re-classification in 1890; she returned to her native waters in Porthmadog for the necessary refit.

Henry Hughes could see the ship from the garden of his home. When he first set eyes on her, she was haggard and worn. He raced down to the quay for a better look. All the marine growth and barnacles of two oceans seemed to have stuck to her sides. Her bottle-green timbers were like Joseph's coat of many colours. The gold strake and the elaborate carving around her stern were shabbily tarnished. The beautiful figurehead was sadly in need of a re-paint. Her decks were secure enough, but the bulwarks, boats, and deck fittings were seriously worn.

Twenty years of incessant hammering by the sea was beginning to tell the inevitable tale, of things wearing out, of wrinkles where once there were smiles. In spite of her vagrant appearance, the townspeople gave her a great ovation and welcome. One Evan Lewis, a local carpenter, said she looked the part that only a fine ship could have played, and that some of his physic would soon bring her round.

The refit started in October and was vigorously continued through the winter. By February, 1890, her seams had been entirely recaulked. New parts had been grafted on where necessary. Putty and pitch filled the minor lacerations in her sides. New copper reached to her loading line. New rigging, spars and sails brought confidence back in her ability to put up more rounds against the demon storms and the punishing heat.

A new fo'c'sle was built on deck to replace the squalid dungeon low down on the forepeak. By February 20th she was like a smartly-dressed middle-aged woman who had been to have her face lifted in an endeavour to keep abreast of her younger rivals,

Two days in to February a certain Dr Evans, who was new to the area, came through the front door of Ceylon Villa, examined Henry's frame after a bout of illness, tapped his chest and pronounced that the best for the boy was to go to sea. Doctors were not to be argued with and before Henry could turn his mind to the thought of missing his school friends, old Captain Griffith sat in the armchair in the front room and went over the necessities of sea sailing. The boy sat on the floor, listening with a mixture of surprise, awe and fear.

The boy happened to know that the freeboard of *Pride of Wales* was three feet. This means that, walking along the main-deck amidships, three feet was the distance down to the surface of the sea. All very well, thought the boy, my grandfather making piles of money out of ship-owning, but this is my life; what about my friends? What about playing sports and having birthday parties? He was being sent out to sea and that could be very far away. His mother would not be there to make him his favourite food and to comfort him. He felt the loneliness and the beginnings of terror.

But he was transplanted. The virtue of sailing was forced upon him. He became a mariner.

He sat in the cabin of *Pride of Wales*. It had mahogany panels with a white ceiling, a decorative skylight in which hung a compass and a paraffin lamp, along with a barometer and clock. Leather settees surrounded a mahogany table. There was a snug copper fireplace with a mirror above the mantelpiece. The captain's berth was built on the starboard side. The chief mate's berth was on the port side. The only light that penetrated these bunks came through the skylight.

On a grey winter morning, in the early 'nineties, Porthmadog harbour presented a scene of unusual activity. The still atmosphere was broken at an early hour by the metallic clank of the dropping prawls of many windlasses. A dozen ships were preparing for sea. The headland known as Pen-y-Bank was topped by wives and children, gathered to wave to their menfolk as they sailed past. Other groups gathered on the quayside to bid godspeed and safe return.

Pride of Wales was the centrepiece. She had visited the port only once before during her life and she was not likely to come again in the next seven years.

The lad gripped the bulwarks. His eyes strayed over the harbour, over to the distant mountains and up the Garth towards his home.

He stepped to the upper topsail halliard and started to pull. The weather-beaten sailors around him started to sing:

> *Santa Ana is going away*
> *Away Santa Ana*
> *Santa Ana is going away*
> *Along the plains of Mexico.*

The two tug boats *Snowdon and* The *Wave of Life* were busily dashing up and down the harbour, tugging the ships from the shallower muddy quays and sending them on their way. There was little hope of this ship floating until the top of the tide. Then the order "Let go the stern rope," was shouted. The anchor was weighed. Hardy sailors manned the windlass and they sang:

> *Blow boys, blow for California O!*
> *There is plenty of gold, so we've been told*
> *On the banks of the Sacramento.*

The ensign was dipped and the poop covered with sailors responding to the shouts of those on the quay.

Pride of Wales was set for Germany with 500 tons of slate, the largest and heaviest single cargo ever carried by ship out of Porthmadog.

The ship passed Ynys Cyngar, crossed the bar and was soon on the high seas. Criccieth Castle was on one side and Harlech Castle on the other. These two sentinels had marked the passing and entrance of hundreds of voyages in the last sixty years or so. But Henry was sea-sick. His stomach heaved as the ship heaved and that night he curled up in his bunk and cried himself to sleep.

They were making for Falmouth. The new rigging had got dangerously slack and other new fittings needed adjusting. Approaching Falmouth they saw many ships pulling at anchor, marine growth on their bellies as evidence of many days at sea. Peering over the sides in clusters were bronzed and bearded man with prominent blue eyes.

The adjustments were made in Falmouth harbour and soon *Pride of Wales* was ready for sailing. Two vessels from Porthmadog had left Falmouth two hours before. The first one passed was the *Ann & Jane Pritchard*; then the brigantine *George Casson*. There was much waving and shouting.

Pride of Wales was sailing for Rio. She passed through the Bay of Biscay without incident. It was a five to six thousand miles trip.

Good weather continued and in about a fortnight's time the NE trade winds were picked up. The ship first ran in to foul weather just off Key West, having emerged from the Gulf of Mexico. Sailors took turns to man the pumps, sometimes waist deep in water.

Dolphins and flying fish decorated the sea. Fish were eaten and dolphins admired for their beauty. Dolphins and sailing ships are companions.

The sun was directly overhead and the ship was becalmed. A feeling of helplessness ran through the crew. The ocean resembled an empty barren waste.

Then the earth seemed to turn, the sea heaving listlessly in huge billows. The ship rolled and it was necessary to lower all the heavy canvas. The top-gallant sails needed rolling and Henry Hughes was being swung to and fro a hundred feet above the sea, holding a rope and a flimsy spar. He got down slowly but safely.

The ship had no set sails. To move about the ship, one had to hang on to ropes. For sleeping, hammocks replaced bunks.

Six days these conditions prevailed. Then, in the distance, a plume of smoke appeared. Soon after a breeze rose. The ship came closer; she was a large French immigrant ship, the *Uruguay*, bound from the River Plate to Marseilles. Just as the breeze reached its height, the immigrants crowded to its side and issued loud cheers. Its siren blew a loud greeting.

Henry Hughes was crossing the Equator for the first time. The Captain stayed up until eight bells and all enjoyed their rum. Olaf said he would tattoo an anchor on Henry's arm to commemorate the event. He took a piece of coal and mashed it to powder, added water to it to make a paste. He took a sailing needle and in the cook's galley, dimly lighted by the cook's lamp, he pierced the design with such skill that it stayed on Henry's arm for the rest of his life.

The arrival at Rio's latitude was on the 57th day after leaving the Elbe. The smell of land was in the air. Coming to watch at noon, Henry was delighted to see a range of mountains off the starboard bow. "Those mountains," said the Captain, "form a part of the Brazilian coast," and pointing to a smooth cone-shaped formation superimposed against the great range," and that is the famous Sugar Loaf mountain, marking the entrance to the most beautiful harbour in the world. But unless some wind comes from somewhere we shall never get there!"

The Welsh phrase *mynyddau Brasil* stayed in Henry's mind.

A large tug-boat called *Emperor* paid a visit. Her dark-skinned skipper, immaculately dressed in white ducks and covered in gold braid, spoke to the Captain in broken English and finally came to the price he wanted for the tow. An agreement was not reached and the foreign vessel left with many curses in the air.

Pride of Wales sailed slowly in to Rio de Janeiro. The many mixed sails had been set with skill and the ship overcame the difficulties of the slight shifting wind and the unpredictable tide. The sky was cloudless, the stars twinkling, as the great ranges towered above and girdled the silent water of this sublime harbour. The glow of the lights of the great city illuminated the sky for miles around.

They had travelled in the region of six thousand miles without seeing any land.

Chapter 33

ON THE OTHER side of the world, in a wet narrow valley in East Bengal, two Welshmen were observing and thinking.

They looked to where the landslip had occurred. It was a V-shaped red shape against the hillside. On one side of it was a platform running around the shoulder of the hill. On this section, part of the new railway had been laid.

Water was dripping from Percy's hat.

The works foreman approached.

"Very bad," he said. "We were digging and then it went down. We lost no men." He was waving his arms in some agitation.

"Well, let's have a closer look."

"What do you think Johnnie?" Percy continued. "Can we get it back by hand labour or is it likely to slip again when it's raining?"

John Williams replied, "Going by the colour of the earth, I'd say it was full of sand. And sand is the enemy of railway foundations, especially on a slope." Echoes of the problems with the Festiniog Railway track up to Blaenau were in his mind.

They walked down the slope and over the stone bridge.

"Tell the men to take an hour off," said Percy to the foreman. He replied with some pleasure.

They walked closer to the landslip.

"I don't like it," said Percy."

"Entirely caused by excess water, I'd say," said John.

"Water coming in quantity down the surface of the hill and having nowhere to go but across the track of our line.

Seems pretty clear. It needs a drainage sluice-gate type of solution."

John pointed to just above the ruined track surface. "It has to be a strong wall. A curved one. And not one tunnel under the line. That would create pressure. We need two tunnels under the line, about twenty feet apart. And above them we need a wall, a very strong one of stone and concrete, curving down at both ends, splitting the torrent of water, taking the pressure off it and directing both sides to the tunnels."

It was a proposal of ingenuity and practicality. It was a solution based on not taking chances. The foremen were gathered and the proposal explained to them in detail.

The rain eased off. Soon the diggers were at the top of the landslide, removing soil from the rear where the wall was to be. Having made footings of some three feet deep, curved, they directed their efforts to digging downwards and sideways and creating two tunnels under the rail track platform.

The instructions had been given. Work was in progress.

"They need direction and they need leadership," said Percy. "We have the solution."

Soon four trucks approached, drawn by stout horses. Stones were unloaded and carried in a line up to the site of the landslip.

"Plenty of concrete," said John. "Especially at the base."

Five days later, the new construction was finished. Nearly a hundred men had worked hard and systematically. The wall was five feet at its highest, of granite and well grouted. Stones had been placed around the entrances to the two tunnels, which had been lined with wood. As they opened on the lower side, stones lined the entrances.

Going back there, both men, now dressed in formal clothes, reluctant to dirty their shoes, praised the work.

"Had this been in England, it would have taken three months. That's after the discussions with officials, drawing maps and so on. That's why they need us. They will get on with whatever we tell them. But we have to be knowledgeable. We have to earn their trust. They look to us for leadership. And when we stop giving it to them, it's time to get out." Percy was very clear about their role.

As they turned away, a shaft of sunlight lit up the valley. It seemed a sign of purpose and achievement.

"Generally, we do good," said Percy.

In their discussions later, they agreed that the railway line from Santahar to Fulchari would be finished in two months' time. And that when it was running, the schedules set and the staff ready in their new uniforms, the trade down towards the mouth of the Ganges would be bigger and faster, and the enormous bay at Chittagong would be even more supplied by ships trading with all parts of the world.

Three month later, the railway line completed and the weather improving, Percy heard that a British sailing ship was approaching Chittagong, intending to pick-up tea. As this had come down from Darjeeling and along the newly-completed railway, Percy set about travelling down to take a look.

He recognised her immediately. She was the same as the one his brother and himself had seen being launched in Borth y Gest. The image on her prow was as bright as ever, with the flowing hair and outstretched hand holding a rose. It was an optimistic sight.

On the quayside were boxes of a size that would fit through the entrance to a ship's hold. Fifty or more men stood around by them. 'These boxes contain high-quality tea,' thought Percy, 'and in each box there are twenty or so fine-mesh sacks, and they must not get wet.'

Hoists on wooden poles were moved in to position. Straps were placed around a box and the lifting began. The boxes swung over the ship, above the trap-door entrance to the hold and carefully lowered, to be pushed in to position by the ship's crew.

'Heading for Ceylon,' thought Percy, 'and then to England'.

The trade in tea from the distant hills had started in earnest. The railway was doing its job. Soon there would be dozens of tea-carrying sailing ships following the excellent start made by the tall, majestic *Pride of Wales.*

Small shops all over Britain would store their tea in tin containers, knee high, with tight-fitting round lids.

'People back home will enjoy their new-quality tea,' thought Percy as he turned away. He had seen the home ship. It was doing its job. That things – the railways and the shipping – were working well was Percy's reward. He left the quayside a happy man.

Chapter 34

FLORENCE HAD set up a career for herself as a lady of society.

Her mother, Annie Louisa Loveday Williams, occupied the house as well, but was little interested in society ladies.

Her brother had married in to the quarry-owning Greaves family and lived in their Maentwrog mansion.

Castell Deudraeth was as grand as ever. Quality of furnishings and decoration had been kept up and the sun shone brightly over the river Dwyryd and over the flowers in the well-kept garden.

There is no doubt that she enjoyed her sister's visits with her four children. Blanche was older now and did not always come. The children were sent in the care of a housemaid. The boy Harold was an active lad. Now in his early teens, he did not seem to be the sort who would join his father's law practice. Every chance he got, he was down at the harbour, mixing with the ship designers and their men, handling the wood, drawing the ropes and engaging in all the activities ship-building encompassed.

The two girls Olive and Edith were bright and charming. In some ways they resembled the previous generation here, when Florence and Blanche sat in the garden on the white seat and had serious conversations.

"Why don't you have a husband, Aunt Florence?" Olive said one morning after breakfast.

It was an innocent, simple question. One that had dozens of implications, mostly not known to the girl.

"What a question!" replied Florence. "My, how do I answer that?"

"It would be nice to have an uncle," pressed Olive. "He would take me for rides. And we would have a picnic."

Olive had an unusual mind for an eleven-year-old. Unlike most children, she knew what was not; she had a sense of something not present and yet might have been present.

"You might have had a young man," she said, precociously.

"I had a young man," said Florence. There was a plaintive look to her face; an emptiness. She also, now, felt what was not.

In her mind, Florence, was struggling. She had a strange vision. It was the colour of sky but it was also the colour of water. As the water got deeper, the colour got darker. She stood, looking at the sky out of the window.

"A young man," repeated Olive, her eyes surveying Aunt Florence's.

"Yes."

"What was his name?"

"Talsarnau … a farm … we would sit with the daffodils … Eifion … His name was Eifion Lloyd Jones." Florence had become tall and quiet. Her eyes were fixed to the upper part of the kitchen wall.

"We would sit with the daffodils," she said again as she lowered her head.

"His parents were lovely. They always welcomed me. They would put out their best china and we would have tea. It was a large farmhouse. They had their own cheese. I used to come back with a pail of milk. Father said they were the salt of the earth. He did not usually take to the small-holders. But these were farmers of the better sort. Generous."

The inevitable question was hanging in the air, and Olive was not too diffident to ask it: "What happened to Eifion?"

There was a silence. The crows could be heard in the trees.

"He didn't have to go to sea," Florence said. "But he had two brothers who were both interested in farming. Eifion was not. He wanted to get out and explore. He often told me that he wished to see London and Paris and Africa. He had seen paintings in books and he wanted to see them. He was a beautiful man."

As Olive looked, tears were flowing from Florence's eyes. They were like small diamonds, catching the light.

"*Carl and Louise* was his ship. She traded in the West Indies and Newfoundland. Built in Borth y Gest by Richard Jones of Garreg Wen, the man who built my sister's ship *Blanche Currey.*"

"But ..." Her eyes turned to the young lady, who was quite still. "But ... She was lost with all hands."

The phrase 'lost with all hands' washed about the room with an icy presence.

"They were heading for Bremen in Germany with slate. The estuary of the river Weser was at high tide. It was night. A storm. A heavy storm."

She paused before delivering her final comment.

"*Carl and Louise* was lost with all hands. We have sacrificed. So many fine young men have been lost."

Florence touched the head of her sister's daughter as she turned to leave the room.

Chapter 35

HAROLD WAS on the quayside on a fine Tuesday morning in February 1891 to witness the launching of the three-masted schooner *Blodwen*.

He had stepped in to the David Jones yard. He saw workmen lining up. Behind them he saw a figure with brown boots and a bowler hat. He was holding a paper up against the ship's timbers. On his left inner arm there was a red weal.

David Jones was familiar with visits by young Harold Currey.

"Is this a good ship?" he asked jocularly of the boy, who was now staring at the timbers.

"Something wrong with them planking," said Harold.

"Oh, and what is that?" said David, hammering his right fist at the timbers. "Very sound. I was just checking the spacings. They seem right."

"But they are flat," said Harold. "They should be over-lapping."

"But, my boy," replied David Jones. "This is not a clinker-built ship."

"Clinker?" enquired Harold.

"Clinker is when you put the plankings over one another. Then you apply caulking to make her watertight."

"So, what is this?" enquired Harold.

"She is carvel-built," said Jones. "Here the planks are edge-up to one another."

"What's the point in that?" asked Harold.

"Faster. Faster through the water. Less to catch the water. A smoother surface. Like a knife through butter. It's my secret weapon," said the small but tough David Jones, laughing.

The new ship was waiting to join its natural partner, the salt water. Miss Maggie Richards of Bryntirion Terrace, Criccieth, stood on the launch platform, bottle in hand. This was the first new ship to be built here after the lull of the eighties. The yard then had to be content with repairing and refitting. But the slate quarries of Blaenau had picked-up and investment once again flowed in to ships. Miss Richards was a member of the family of Messrs. Richards and Company, shipowners and shipbrokers of Porthmadog, who, together with Captain John Roberts, Glanmeirion, Talsarnau, had placed the order for the new vessel with David Jones.

"I name this ship, *The Blodwen*," came the clear voice from the platform. The new ship was placed at a good angle and down the slip she went. A frothy ripple spread from her as she hit the water, to the delighted shouting of the dozens who had gathered about the quay to witness this important event.

"She floats," said David Jones, throwing his arms in the air. "The first. Three cheers for *The Blodwen*." Voices joined in, hats were thrown in the air, and on the adjacent shipyard of David Williams, the builders of the *Dorothy* kept a diplomatic silence.

Chapter 36

CHARLES EDWIN SPOONER, third son of the late Charles Easton Spooner, was at breakfast. The white tablecloth and the bone china had been laid with precision.

Amir came in, holding an envelope. He laid it on the table, next to the plate carrying the egg-shell which had been cut open with a sharp knife.

"Mail delivery," said Amir. "Tall man on a bicycle."

"Thank you," said Charles Edwin.

He noticed the typewritten address and the 'Esquire' after his name.

"Official delivery. From the Offficial Residence," he said. He wondered what it was about.

Opening the envelope, he found a thick white leaf of paper with a black printed address in the top centre.

The letter was from Henry Logue-Harrison. It requested his presence at ten-thirty the following morning.

So, the following morning in the pink house at the back of Colombo he found himself in conversation with Henry.

"You came to the Survey Department, Ceylon, in nineteen-seventy-six. You were transferred to the Public Works Department, where you have been this fourteen years," said Henry, who had checked, to get his facts right.

"You have served this island with distinction. You have created a structure through which progress has been possible. You have sat down with your chosen officials, bringing on local people to Management. You have shown them how a properly-managed structure can work. Now you have ten men who can take over from you. Some are railway specialists, others roads, others town planners. And you have managed water and sewage. You have created work for thousands of natives. All is orderly and positive and much respected."

Henry paused. He could see that Charles Edwin was waiting for the conclusion of this praise.

"And now, we want you to do it somewhere else. To take your talents to another country. To Malaya."

Charles Edwin had never been there. He had heard about it. Mostly about how primitive it was. Undeveloped. No proper roads or railways.

He looked at Henry with blandness and curiosity.

Henry said, "I realise this is a shock. To uproot you, from your friends and connections. But Straits Settlements is desperately in need of good men. We cannot administer, we cannot manage at all, unless we have ways and means of communicating and distributing and travelling. The climate is challenging. The landscape is rough, the terrain makes it difficult to get from one place to another. But if anyone can do it, you can."

"What is my role, my job, and its title?" asked Charles Edwin.

"It is State Engineer of Selangor," he replied. "Selangor is the richest area. And State Engineer covers everything from railways to roads to buildings to water. You will have your hands full."

Charles Edwin was beginning to rise to the task. He relished a challenge. His main concern was with his household. He would not sell the house. He would not put his friends out of a home. He would make arrangements with Assif and Amir such that they could all stay there.

"Very well," he said. "My duty is calling."

"Good man," said Henry. "I shall write it out for you. I shall arrange for you to travel in two weeks' time."

He stood up from his chair. The window behind him showed a long view of Colombo with the sea in the background.

His last words to Charles Edwin were again, "Good man," as he shook his hand.

Chapter 37

IN THE EARLY 1890s, Prussia Street, Liverpool, was a centre of Welsh life. Aspects of it gleamed – its clean windows, its paintwork and the three steps up to the front door. Families here had Welsh names: there were Joneses, Morrises, Davieses and so on and when the lady of the house, her apron newly washed and her hair tied up around her head, got on her knees with her bucket, scrubbing-brush and block soap (made in nearby Port Sunlight), she dedicated herself to her task to the extent of not naming her neighbours by their Christian names but uttering "Mrs Morris" and suchlike when her neighbour appeared. Children ran up and down the street; they played with a ball, skipped and played hopscotch. And every now and then a Welsh phrase was heard – *"paid a dweud"*; *"cau dy geg"* and the assertive *"diawl"* – all because their families spoke the language, and if the father was a sailor, new words, some of distant places, were added – *"Rio"*, *"Port"*, *"Boston"*, *"Phosphate"*.

Standing in the top window of the most westerly of Prussia Street houses, you could look over King Edward Street to Princes Dock, the tops of masts of schooners showing above slate roofs and chimney-pots.

Nothing cheered the street more than the sight of a sailor fresh from the sea turning the corner at the end of the road, carrying his belongings in his canvas bag on his back. He was often whistling or singing. The children paused at their games and stood to face him, some asking questions.

In January 1892 *Pride of Wales* was 22 years old. At high tide she sailed surely in to Princes Dock. She had nine crew, under Captain Griffith, with Evan Pugh, mate. The dock was surrounded by storage buildings, built close to the quay wall. Sailing ships could get in there but steam ships were too large for the dock gate, so the age of sail continued vigorously in the old part of Liverpool. Welshmen came here to take to sea and Prussia Street housed many a young man from north Wales who rented a bed for a few nights, looking to be hired.

One centre of hiring sailors was the 'Vaults' pub in Vauxhall Street. Evan Pugh knew this and in the second evening after docking he walked over there to enjoy his beer and see if there were any men looking for a hiring on *Pride of Wales*.

As he leaned against the bar, he was approached by a young man:

"Are you hiring?" he enquired.

"If the quality is there," was the reply.

"I am Guto, from Abersoch. My auntie lives in Liverpool. I am a hard worker."

"Can you take a long voyage?" Evan Pugh enquired. "Have you sailed the high seas?"

"Have sailed to Hamburg, from Caernarfon. And two times to Amsterdam."

"Well, are you an able seaman?" quizzed Evan. "And can you put up with the cold, the wind, the ship's movement?"

Guto replied, "I am an Abersoch man. Cold winds out there. My father too is from Abersoch. Farming stock. Lleyn. Thin soil and stone walls."

Evan Pugh thought that sea-going wasn't much better, but there were good times, when the sea was calm and the wind friendly.

"Sails. Handle sails? Good strong hands. Let me see."

He took both of Guto's hands, turned them over.

"*Iawn. Dwylo mawr.*" [Good. Large hands].

There was a pause. Evan Pugh looked in to the young man's eyes.

"You are hired for a long voyage on *Pride of Wales*, starting Wednesday. Report to Princes Dock at one p.m."

Then the same evening, in the next two hours, two more men were hired, so the three men who had been signed-off after The *Pride of Wales's* last voyage had now been replaced.

Evan was not one for niceties. If the man looked right, he was right. You looked at the shoulders, the hands and the eyes.

Captain J.J.Griffith set a leaf of paper before him, dipped his pen in ink and wrote the following letter:

My Dear Harry,

I have been given to understand from the Owner that you have decided not to come with me this voyage. The fact that we are going to Santos is given as the reason. Well, I cannot blame you, nor those who have probably influenced you in this respect. Santos is a most unpleasant place, and as you know I have cause to remember and despise it – my pitted face will for all time bear witness of its horrors. On the eve of sailing I thought I would like to write to wish you good luck and to tell you how much I shall miss your cheerful companionship. The old cabin where we have been together so long cannot quite be the same. Somehow I am not looking forward to this trip. I am beginning to feel the strain that these long ocean voyages in small ships entail, and *Pride of Wales* is getting no younger, as you know ...

Do write me from time to time and post me up in news of yourself and your movements.

My greeting to your people,

Yours very sincerely,

J.J.Griffith

PS Bob is coming with us again, and of course Nancy Wellington.

Pride of Wales left Liverpool during February, 1892, bound for Santos, South America, with a general cargo.

She arrived in Santos, south of Rio de Janeiro, Brazil, in April. It was a desolate scene. Ships of many sizes and sorts lay at anchor, many of them empty of crew. Yellow fever and smallpox had raced through the human population, and marooned at harbour under the burning sun, ships had been devastated.

Each day the crew of *Pride of Wales* wished for wind, to get them out of there, but none came until many weeks later. One after another, including Evan Pugh, the crew fell ill and died.

Eventually there was a little wind and the ship left harbour with a replacement crew and pulled in to Monte Cuyo, in Mexico. Here she loaded about 350 tons of logwood for Fleetwood, England.

Sailing north-east and abreast of Bermuda, a huge storm blew up. Her position was 40' 40*N 37'20*W.

Two of her inexperienced crew were washed overboard and drowned.

Then her bowsprit and jib-boom were torn asunder by the force of the storm.

Then her foremast was blown away.

The hole in her bow was letting in sea-water which could not be pumped out.

She was gradually sinking.

Her sailors were looking-out for help. "Sail" came the shout from aloft. A Norwegian barque had seen them and turned in their direction. Through their telescope they could see Captain Griffiths and six of his crew huddled in the after-part of the ship. As the Norwegians approached, arms were raised in the air.

Stores, with great difficulty, were transferred from the sinking ship to the floating one. Fresh water had to be carried over.

When Captain Griffiths last saw *Pride of Wales*, her head

sinking lower in to the sea, she appeared to be kneeling in prayer. She was left to perish.

Guto, from Abersoch, survived. He went back to his father's farm and never went to sea again.

Chapter 38

Kuala Lumpur

INSIDE THE Lake Gardens park there are two hills on which there are two large residences. One is named 'Carcosa' and the other 'Seri Negara'.

The former was built as the official residence of Sir Frank Athelstane Swettenham, High Commissioner of Malaya, who in the 1890s was Resident-General of the Federated Malay States. The house was, according to Sir Frank, "...was designed and built for me at Kuala Lumpur by the late Mr C.E.Spooner, assisted by Mr A.B.Hubback ..."

Arthur Hubback was a military man through and through. He had an upright stance, and always wore a stiff upright collar and a three-piece suit, usually in tweed.

"But you are not the official architect," he said to Charles Edwin Spooner as they sat on the veranda of the Hubbock house, over the park's pretty blue lake.

"No. Charles Norman is the official man. But frankly, he hasn't much idea. Plans and sketches go through his hands but largely I draw them or have them drawn. There are some excellent native draughtsmen here. Sometimes I just put my name on the designs. I can't do all of it. I haven't the time. But I get them done. And down there in the Resident-General's building there are cases full of excellent drawings, all done by me or a member of my team."

"But, this means you really are the official architect," said Arthur, who despite the rigour and stiffness of his role in the military, had quite an enquiring, perceptive, mind.

"I don't make too much of it, in case somebody comes up

against it and makes a nuisance. My office is large and cool. I have nearly a dozen young men working there. We deal with public works. We see that the roads and bridges are sound and we build new ones. We see that land has proper ownership and that this is marked on paper. We plan new towns, marking where houses are to be built. And we want houses of proper quality, not these dreadful mud huts we see everywhere. We need to encourage the business of building and have rules for foundation-laying. Water drainage is a major factor in a climate like this, when sometimes the rains come down in torrents. We begin with large drainage pipes, otherwise everything would be swept away.." So, the Spooner practicality in design and engineering was evident. It was virgin territory. It needed a sure pair of hands.

The two men admired the two buildings. They had a beautiful light about them. The front elevation of 'Carcosa' was divided in to balconies and a veranda with open spaces faced with pillars with curved tops. One side of the building was built outwards, enclosing a large balcony, with a decorated handrail. The view was magnificent, over the park with the sea in the distance.

"I have made this Indian-style," said Charles Edwin. "Or, perhaps, Malay-style. A people should have their style. It is their legacy and way of thinking. No good putting our style on them. This is not Florence or Paris or London. The style comes from the climate and the culture."

"Wasn't there a fire here?" asked Hubback.

"Back in the eighties," replied Edwin. "Ravaged the place. After that Frank Swettenham insisted on all new building should be built in brick and tile. Quite right too. We now have the Sanitary Board. We don't want those terrible diseases, cholera and suchlike. This city is changing. We have insisted on good standards of building. Soon it will be the capital of the Federated Malay States."

"And in the centre we have the huge new build. Have you seen it? The New Government Office. It deserves a better name. I have worked on its design. Norman drew the ground plan, but a young man in my office called Bidwell did all the detailed elevations, and jolly good he was at it; a real find. He seemed to understand Mohametan style. In its centre there is a huge clock tower with a copper dome:e large quantities of brick and copper and plaster in the building. The local workers are working on it as if there is no tomorrow. They are very proud of it. The final cost will be over one hundred thousand Straits Dollars. When it's finished we shall move all the government offices in there."

As they moved indoors, Arthur Hubback knew that Charles Edwin Spooner was the man for the job. He was in his element.

The spirit of his father was in him.

Chapter 39

IN APRIL 1907 David Williams, shipbuilder, received an account from Jones and Morris, sailmakers. On the 19th he settled the account relating to "… to contract New Outfit of Sails for the New Three masted Sr building, all complete with covers, Tarpaulins as per specification at Lump sum price £118."

'Owen Owens should be pleased,' thought David Williams 'for these are of exceptional quality.'

The ship on the stocks was the *R.J.Owens*, built for Owen Owens of Borthwen, Borth y Gest.

'This name is my home, the white bay,' thought Owen Owens. He had sailed successfully and in distant ports he had imagined the village of his birth, facing the sea, its bay filling and emptying each day. It became his ambition to have a house built there.

Facing the estuary, Borthwen was one of the first to be built in a crescent around the bay. Next to the house was a lane leading to a yard where Owen kept his larger belongings, including a wooden skiff. When he felt the need to clear his head, he dragged it out on its trolley which he rolled down the shingle and when safely launched at high tide he handled the oars with vigour and symmetry, directing the boat in the direction of Harlech and making a circle in the estuary before returning. This little trip had the extra advantage of showing him how the sands had shifted, making his trip out to sea as cptain of a schooner somewhat safer.

He had held on to his money and this time he invested in 32 of the 64 shares issued against the new ship. Humphrey Owens, his father, who lived in 'Pilots Houses' at the peak of the bay, had eight shares. Other shares were held by locals, including John Thomas Jones, Bank Manager of Porthmadog and William Morris, ship's chandler.

Owen appreciated how his father, who had been a tight man all his life, had showed such faith in him and his new ship to buy such a number of shares. His brother John, also a sailor, of Borth y Gest, held 4 shares, so that between the three of them they held 44 shares. Managing owner of the *R.J.Owens* was the shipbroker Griffith Pritchard of Bod Hyfryd, Penrhyndeudraeth, who held 4 shares; so all the practical details were to be ship-shape.

The new ship was David Williams's masterpiece. As she was being built on the *cei* in Porthmadog, she attracted admiring glances. It was as if she had a life in her; as if she had already grown through the period of childhood and being a young lady and had just arrived at that stage of development when a woman emerges. She was slim, elegant and symmetrical. She had three masts, each with a fore-and-aft main sail. Her three main sails hung from stout spars which rose upwards at an angle from the masts and on her foremast were two square-sail gaffs, the top one a double. Her main mast was taller than the others, and hung on it, and on the mizzen were spars designed to support further square sails. Attached to her bowsprit were her jib sail, then a foresail. She was fully prepared. Sailed properly by sailors who understood the rigging, she was as effective a sailing ship as could be.

In the parlour of Borthwen, Borth y Gest, inside the front window, was a Bible, resting on a highly-polished mahogany table. It measured some ten inches across and twelve inches upwards. It was covered with mid-brown calfskin, with reinforced edges. On the upper side, from the outer edge, were two brass spigots and from the lower edge rose two brass hinges which when raised and clipped on the spikes, kept the Bible tight and safe.

Opening the Bible, Owen observed his small neat

handwriting in the right and left hand margins. Each entry carried a date, a map reading, the name of the ship and its location. Owen was a meticulous man. When at sea, he kept the Bible in a waterproof box strapped on a high shelf in his cabin, and when he came ashore he would wrap it in linen and carry it safely in his valise.

Born in 1870, in a room overlooking the Glaslyn, Owen first went to sea in the large Nefyn two-masted schooner *Miss Thomas*, engaged in the Baltic and Moroccan trades. By 1895 he was aboard the *Venedocian*, and it was aboard her, at Gibraltar, that he started entering notes in his Bible. On 30 October 1895 he recorded that he had read the fourth chapter of Malachi. He then served on the *Laura Griffith* and the *Dorothy*. Entries from Cape St. Vincent and Cadiz followed. In October 1898 the *Dorothy* (built by Griff and David Williams) was at Black Tickle, Labrador. He then became an Able Seaman aboard the *Beeswing* and in November 1899 this ever-brave little ship rounded the hostile Cape Horn and sailed some two thousand miles up the coast of Chile, to finally dock in Taltal, which is up to the north of this long-stretching coastal country.

If you were in the front room of Borthwen, Borth y Gest and you opened this Bible, you might fancy that you smelled – or imagined – the odours and sounds of exotic and not-so-exotic far-away places.

In 1898 Owen Owens became Second Mate on a steel barque of large size, the *Norfolk Island*. In December 1900 at Melbourne he recorded that he had started re-reading the New Testament. Owen then signed as mate on the *Ednyfed* and was at Newcastle, New South Wales, and then across the Pacific, round the Horn again and up the coast of South America to Salaverry which is in Peru. This was 1903.

How can we imagine these voyages, these enormous distances, sailed in a ship with no motor power? Dependent entirely on the skill of the Captain in plotting direction and calculating distances, always under threat from the weather, reliant on the skill of seamen (many of them no older than sixteen) handling canvas, ropes and rigging, sometimes a hundred feet in the air, these ships reached their distant destinations with an accuracy and sureness which borders on the miraculous.

How can we imagine a team of committed boatbuilders, on a muddy bank in Porthmadog, creating a vessel strong and reliable enough to counter the stresses of the sea, the winds, over these enormous distances.

His Bible records a visit to Taltal, Chile, again; his fine writing reads, "… off Cape Horn running before a heavy westerly gale and high seas bound from Taltal, Chile, to Rotterdam with nitrate …" The distance was over eight thousand miles.

He came home and he put his money in to a new ship, one of the Porthmadog pedigree. They had proved their worth on the seas of the world.

For the maiden voyage of the *R.J.Owens*, Captain Owen Owens had Humphrey Owens, his brother, in the crew, along with another Borth y Gest man, Bob Morris. 'Bob Ship' was his Mate and Griffith Roberts, boatswain. A young man from Amlwch; an eighteen-year-old ordinary seaman from Hamburg; and two sixteen-year-old boys from Criccieth (who gave their addresses as Marine Crescent) comprised the rest of the crew.

The *R.J.Owens* was at Papenburg in May, 1907, Oporto in June, thence to Cadiz and then across the Atlantic to St John's, Newfoundland by 24 July, The Bible records that she was off Cape St. Frances, Labrador, on 5 August. This ship then turned to face the Atlantic again and arrived at Lisbon on 12 October. She berthed at Patras on the 11th of November. She moved on to Seville and on the 26th of January, 1908, was on her way to Amlwch where she arrived on the 20th of February.

Captain Owens remained. His ship was the pinnacle of ship-building achievement. She regularly sailed the

Newfoundland-MediterraneanB route, often carrying salt westwards and codfish eastwards in order to satisfy those Catholics who ate fish on a Friday. In May 1909, the *R.J.Owens* sailed from Hull to Gibraltar, Cadiz, Newfoundland, Labrador, Genoa, Huelva and home to Porthmadog by March 1910. Two of her crew gave their addresses as Limekiln Lane, Porthmadog: one was a native of New South Wales; the other was born in Launcesron, Tasmania.

Captain Owen's Bible entries noted that he and his ship visited Shoal Bay, Labrador on 29 August 1909. On the voyage starting at Llanelli in June 1911, a new name appears on the crew list, "Ellen Mary Owen, aged 24, of Brookside, Criccieth," who signed as "First Ship, Stewardess." The master's wife left the ship at Lisbon shortly before she sailed for Cadiz, thence to Nippers Harbour, Newfoundland, back to Gibraltar, Patras, Civita Vecci, Preston and home to Porthmadog in April 1912.

After further crossings of the North Atlantic, Owen Owens, in January 1914, was succeeded as Captain of the *R.J.Owens* by Captain Evan Evans of Pwllheli.

With the outbreak of the First World War, the locally held crew agreement lists of the *R.J.Owens* cease.

On June 20, 1916, she was sold to James Ryan of St.John's, Newfoundland.

She was wrecked in July, 1917. That terrible year. The year of Passchendaele. The year Hedd Wyn died at Ypres.

In April 1917 at Arras, Edward Thomas died before his collected poems came out, his body untouched and unscarred, killed by the turbulent air of a passing shell

Captain Owen Owens, who had made dozens of Atlantic and Pacific crossings in his magnificent ship, aged thirty-eight, one dark night fell to his death. He had stepped off a quayside to a ship below, at low tide. He was serving on a steam ship. But it could be surmised that in that late evening, his mind clouded by tiredness, he thought he was still in Porthmadog, stepping from the quayside on to the deck of a native sailing-ship, whose deck would be only some two feet below the level of the quay. Instead, a new development killed him. The steam ship was not a sailing ship and its deck was some ten feet lower.

Chapter 40

And, finally

Charles Edwin Spooner died at Kuala Lumpur on the 14th of May, 1909. In his latter years he served as General Manager of the Federated Malay States Railways. Spooner Road, in Singapore, is named after him.

***

George Percival Spooner worked on management of railways in East Bengal, India, now Bangladesh.

He returned to Britain, penniless, and lived in London where he worked as a Special Constable. The fate of his wife and child is not known.

***

William Williams, Superintendent of Railways, Festiniog Railway, died 23 December 1915 at his home in New Street, Porthmadog. His son John Williams attended his funeral. He had returned to Britain after retiring from the East Bengal Railway in 1915.

***

John Williams's son, Edwin Williams, worked in forestry in India during the Raj, retiring to live in Dwygyfylchi, Penmaenmawr. He died in October 1965. He is buried at Penmorfa, Porthmadog.

***

... restless wave ... mighty oceans deep ... in peril on the sea ...

The Borth y Gest brig *Blanche Currey* was converted to a schooner in Liverpool in 1894.

On a voyage from Bahia, Brazil to Newfoundland, she was lost off Cape Race with all hands during February, 1914. This was 22 months after the sinking of the *Titanic* in the same general area.

* * *

The three-masted schooner *Gestiana*, built by David Williams of 15 Madoc Street, Porthmadog, was launched on June 5, 1913. She had to be launched 'broadside on'. On a day of low cloud and a cold wind, a Union flag attached to her bowsprit, she splashed in to the waters of the harbour without her masts and rigging because of the confined space across the harbour.

Most of her shareholdings were owned by residents of Blaenau Ffestiniog and Penrhyndeudraeth. Many were quarry owners or workers. Margaret Lloyd George, wife of David Lloyd George of Bron Awelon, Criccieth, owned one share. As the wife of the great man, who had started his extraordinary career in politics (as the arch persuader) in the streets of this town, she was invited to launch this new ship.

It was 1913. It was before the advent of World War One. It was a gloomy day.

The lady, dressed in black with a fur collar and large hat, swung the bottle at the ship's bow. It hit. It did not break.

The onlookers looked at one another.

David Williams, perhaps more familiar with the hard ribs of his vessel, took the bottle in his right hand, holding it as a policeman might hold a truncheon, and brought it crashing down.

There was a cheer.

Later, after being fully fitted and finished, the *Gestiana* sailed on her first voyage.

She ran aground on Goodwin Sands on her first voyage from Dysart, Scotland, was re-floated and sailed on to Newfoundland and thence to Nova Scotia.

She was overtaken by a heavy storm and driven ashore at Gooseberry Cove, near Brig Lorraine, Cape Breton, Nova Scotia, on Saturday, 4 October 1913.

The crew were rescued by Seaman J.N. Myonis jumping on rocks and getting a line ashore.

The vessel broke up and was a total wreck.

Myonis, a Newfoundland seaman, had joined the *Gestiana* some seven weeks previously.

No more ships were built in Porthmadog/Borth y Gest.

* * *

In less than twelve months, Britain was at war with Germany; Porthmadog vessels were trapped in the Elbe; the slate trade ceased.

* * *

On the edge of Porthmadog, up a lane on the left of the Criccieth road, just beyond the second entrance to the industrial park, is the Mariners Cemetery. Approaching it, the atmosphere is dark, under overhanging trees, but its entrance looks in to the sun. Behind the sloping plot, the traditional pale green and light orange hues of the ragged fields and old stone walls run up the slope of Moel-y-Gest, as if holding and supporting the place with a very local sympathy. There are hundreds of graves, some marked with a slate headstone displaying an image of a schooner or an anchor. Other plots are more elaborate, with marble and iron railings, now rusty.

Some of the graves have fresh flowers on them.

Looking back at these rows on rows of graves, one

wonders how many contain the remains of bodies? Or do they contain rotting coffins and in them stones, rubble, with the weight of a body?

* * *

One part of a Porthmadog ship has survived. On the muddy banks of the river Torridge in north Devon are the remains – consisting of upstanding oak timbers – of the *M.A.James*, a Western Ocean Yachts schooner, built by David Williams in Porthmadog in 1900.

finis